James Walker

Memoir of Josiah Quincy

James Walker

Memoir of Josiah Quincy

ISBN/EAN: 9783337733902

Printed in Europe, USA, Canada, Australia, Japan

Cover: Foto ©Raphael Reischuk / pixelio.de

More available books at **www.hansebooks.com**

MEMOIR

OF

JOSIAH QUINCY.

BY

JAMES WALKER, D.D.

From the " Proceedings of the Massachusetts Historical Society"

FOR 1866-1867.

CAMBRIDGE:

PRINTED BY JOHN WILSON AND SON.

1867.

MEMOIR

OF

JOSIAH QUINCY.

EDMUND QUINCY, the emigrant ancestor of the Quincy family
in this country, came from Achurch, Northamptonshire, England. He arrived here Sept. 4, 1633, in the same vessel with
the Rev. John Cotton, and several laymen "of good estate."

His descendants have not been numerous; but, as many of
them were educated men and in public life, the name has
always been distinguished. Josiah Quincy, jun., so called because he died in the lifetime of his father, and because his
name thus written is indissolubly associated with the early
struggles which led to American Independence, was of the
fifth generation. He was then a young lawyer in Boston,
rapidly rising into note. Of an ardent temperament, jealous
for the rights and liberties of the Colonies, bold, eloquent,
incorruptible, he was eminently fitted to become a leader in
the impending Revolution. He was married, in October, 1769,
to Abigail Phillips, the eldest daughter of William Phillips,
one of the most distinguished and successful of the Boston
merchants of that day. They resided in Washington (then
Marlborough) Street, nearly opposite the old Province House,
where was born, Feb. 4, 1772, their son Josiah, the subject of
the following memoir.

In the autumn of 1774, the father embarked for England, in the hope of serving his country abroad, and at the same time recruiting his own health, which had begun to give way under the pressure of professional and public cares. The first part of this hope was fulfilled, but not the second; he died on his passage home, April 26, 1775, only a few hours before the ship entered the harbor of Gloucester. The battle of Lexington had taken place in the preceding week; Boston was occupied by the British troops, and all intercourse with the country suspended. For this reason, the inhabitants of Gloucester proceeded to bury him with such marks of respect as the times would permit.* Everywhere, as a cotemporary tells us, "the multitude of the people were his mourners;" and he is still remembered with that peculiar interest which attaches to a proto-martyr, especially when, as in this case, he is cut off in the midst of a career of great promise.

On sailing from Boston, eight months before, he had left his wife in charge of the family, which then consisted of a son and a daughter. She had remained in town for some time after its military occupation by General Gage, being detained by the dangerous illness of both of these children. The daughter died April 13; after which, with her son, she hastened to join her parents, who, in the distracted state of the country in and about Boston, had retired to Norwich, in Connecticut. Here she received the intelligence of her husband's death,—a great sorrow, which cast its shadow over her whole subsequent life. All the accounts of this lady which have come down to us, represent her as being one of the most esteemed and attractive persons in the elevated circle in which she moved. But the heart of the young widowed mother was never weaned from its first love. "She survived her husband three and twenty years; his fame and memory being the chief solace of her life, and the perfect

---

* His remains were afterwards removed to the burial-ground in Quincy.

fulfilment of parental duty to their surviving child, its only object."*

With this child, who had then just completed his third year, she continued to make part of her father's family, not only during his stay at Norwich, but after his return to Boston, until her son entered college. It was probably the circumstance that she thus had no proper home of her own, which made her less averse to placing him at a public school at the early age of six. Other things also conspired to recommend the step. The school proposed was Phillips Academy, in Andover, which her uncle and her cousin of that place, with the assistance of her father, had just founded. There he would always be near, and under the constant supervision of, those relatives; and there, also, the mother, in her frequent visits to them, would have opportunity to watch over his progress. The Academy was first opened April 30, 1778; and young Quincy was admitted early in the following month, his name standing the twenty-seventh on its roll.

During the eight years of his connection with that seminary, he boarded with the clergyman of the parish, the Rev. Mr. French. Such were the kindnesses and indulgences he there met with, that, in after-life, he always looked back on the Andover parsonage as a second home, and indeed as the only real home of his boyhood.† But, as might be presumed from the extreme youth of the pupil, things did not get on so well for some time in the school-room. The preceptor was Eliphalet Pearson, afterwards a professor in Harvard College, and at a later period in Andover Theological Institution,—a strict and vigorous disciplinarian of the old régime. Mr. Quincy, in a letter written not many years before his death, gives the following account of the methods adopted by this teacher, and of their effect on himself:—

---

* "Memoir of the Life of Josiah Quincy, jun., by his Son," p. 29.

†. For a full account of his obligations to the family, see Mr. Quincy's letter to Dr. Sprague, in "Annals of the American Pulpit," vol. ii. pp. 44-48.

"He had the confidence of the parents and the public from his thoroughness. No boy was permitted to learn B, before he was perfect in all the relations of A. I was a great hand at marbles, and hunting the striped squirrel from the Academy to the parsonage; but, as to hunting down the pages of Cheever's Accidence, then our first book, I had neither will nor power. But there was the rule, — you must be perfect in it. I was kept in that book the whole of my seventh, and part of my eighth, year, until it was odious to me; and even now the very name of Cheever is, to my imagination, something of an *ogre*. Dr. Pearson's discipline was strict and severe, and, though naturally of a kind temperament, he governed by fear. It was the fashion of the time, imported from England, and thought to be essential to the advancement of learning. Dr. Pearson was a full convert to it, and an expert practitioner. I must be excused from writing on this point, as it would compel me *renovare dolores*. But, though a great sufferer under the ancient system of discipline, I must say it had some advantages over the modern."

The boy's progress in his studies for two or three years being slow, his teacher advised his mother to give up the plan of sending him to college. Happily for him, and happily for the College, she was not so easily discouraged. In due time, the natural development of his faculties, and of his characteristic energy and determination to succeed, began to put him in better relations with his books. A few months before he left the Academy, Dr. Pearson was called to a professorship at Cambridge; his place as preceptor being supplied by Dr. Ebenezer Pemberton, an experienced teacher of much repute in those days.* Under the instructions of this gentleman, he completed his preparatory course, and entered Harvard College in 1786, at the age of fourteen. There he immediately took a high position as a scholar, and, though one of the youngest in the class, graduated, in 1790, with its first honors.

---

* Ebenezer Pemberton, LL.D., grandson of the Old South pastor of the same name, had received his education in the College of New Jersey, and had been a teacher in that colony. President Madison and Aaron Burr are said to have been among his early pupils.

Immediately after graduating, he began the study of law in the office of the Hon. William Tudor, then a leading member of the Boston bar. His mother, as already intimated, had taken a house of her own when he entered college, that he might have an independent home in his vacations. The house was in Court Street, on ground now occupied by Tudor's Building. She resided there until after he had become a student at law, and then removed to a house in Federal Street, the site of which, with the garden, is now Sullivan Place. Soon afterward she established herself in a more spacious and eligible mansion, situated on the corner of Pearl and High Streets, which her father purchased in 1792 of the executors of Mr. Merchant; and there she continued to reside until her death. Meanwhile her son had completed his legal studies in the summer of 1793, and was admitted to the bar. At the Commencement in the same year, he also took his second degree at Harvard; and, according to a custom of that day, delivered what was then called "The Masters' Oration," his subject being "The Ideal Superiority of the Present Age in Literature and Politics."

Mr. Quincy was now twenty-one. His education, both academical and professional, had been accomplished, not only creditably, but with distinction; his family connections placed him at once in the best society, and he was looked upon as a young man of large expectations; to all which must be added, a handsome person, full of life and health. Yet it was at this age and in these circumstances that we find him laying down for himself a strict and almost stoical rule of life and duty. "It is not," he writes to a classmate, soon after they had left college, "it is not the natural brilliancy of wit and the flashes of imagination (which, by the world, is denominated genius) that are, in my opinion, to be envied. It is firmness of nerve, — that strength of mind which capacitates us for intense application and hard, laborious attention, — which is the soil where every laurel and every virtue is cultivated with

success." He affixed to his study-table, that it might be continually before his eyes, the following epigraph from Cicero:
*Præclare Socrates hanc viam ad gloriam proximam et quasi
compendiariam dicebat esse; si quis id ageret, ut, qualis haberi
vellet, talis esset.* And, to show how thoroughly his principles were carried into effect, a single anecdote will suffice.
When a young lawyer in Boston, he joined a party who met
at a fixed hour in the morning to play billiards, for exercise
and amusement merely. He was fond of the game, and soon
found he was looking at his watch to see if the appointed
hour had arrived. This disposition alarmed him; he feared
he should become too much interested in games of skill or
chance, and immediately left the party and never met them
again, notwithstanding the raillery of his associates.

That such a man would succeed in whatever he seriously
undertook, was as certain as any thing can be in this world.
What would have been the degree of his success in the law,
if he had given himself wholly to it, and continued in it long
enough to compete for its highest distinctions and rewards,
we have no means of determining; for his attention was soon
called away to politics and public life. He is understood
to have regretted in after-years the last-mentioned circumstance; but, as it would seem, without reason. He undoubtedly yielded to the promptings of his nature; and these,
when distinctly pronounced, are the best guide in such cases.
And, besides, it is easy to see that his mind, though active on
all subjects, was better fitted for that kind of activity which
has to do with affairs, than with that which has to do with
the settlement of principles and rules, or the investigation of
truth. Then, too, he was his father's son; and there was this
clause in his father's will: "I give to my son, when he shall
arrive to the age of fifteen years, Algernon Sidney's Works,
John Locke's Works, Lord Bacon's Works, Gordon's Tacitus, and Cato's Letters. May the spirit of liberty rest upon
him!"

Under these influences, it is not strange that his thoughts and his ambition were early turned to the State. Meanwhile the community had begun to be agitated by novel and exciting questions, which threatened, in the opinion of many, the stability of our free institutions.* The contested adoption of the Constitution by the several States had given rise to the Federal and Democratic parties; and the antagonism thus occasioned was more and more intensified by the different views entertained in this country of the French Revolution, as it went on from one excess to another. All Mr. Quincy's convictions and tastes and associations inclined him to the conservative or Federal side, as representing the American idea of liberty, in contradistinction to the French idea of liberty. And, as it was not his habit to do things by halves or with reserves, he at once became an active member of the party, and from that time identified its interests with those of the whole people, and never wavered in his loyalty to it, through good report and through evil report. "To the day of his death," as his son has told us, "he professed and called himself a Federalist, and nothing else. Though, after the dispersion of the Federal party, he voted for the candidates of different parties, according to his estimation of their merits, he never regarded himself as belonging to any of them, — not even to the Republican party of his old age, though he gave

---

* As early as 1792, Mr. Quincy wrote to a friend what may now be regarded as prophecy. After noticing the disorder and violence attending at that time an election in New York, he goes on: "Whether Clinton has the advantage of Jay, or the Chief Justice of the Governor, neither you nor I have the materials or the inclination to decide. But if such animosity can be excited, such tumults fomented, by a dispute concerning the governmental chair of a single State, what will in some future period result from passions equally strong, minds in all probability less well-regulated, and numbers immensely increased, when roused by the claimants of a four-years' crown, with their blood rising in proportion to the dignity and importance of the office; when the South shall crown an Eumenes, and the North an Antipater. If such materials so disposed do not raise a conflagration, if such opportunities do not excite a Catiline to blow about the seeds of contention, or a Faux to apply a torch to this combustible pile, it will be because nature, or its God, has new-modelled the constitution of man. Our country seems to have this issue upon trial, — Whether man has virtue sufficient to restrain liberty from running into licentiousness."

2

his vote and the weight of his influence to its candidates and
its policy." *

Mr. Quincy was married June 6, 1797, to Eliza Susan
Morton. Her father, Colonel John Morton, was a wealthy
merchant in New York at the breaking out of the War of
Independence. He was a zealous patriot, so liberal in his
loans to the Government as to be called by the British, "The
Rebel Banker," by which his own fortune was considerably
impaired. He had now been dead sixteen years. His widow,
the bride's mother, resided in a house at the corner of Pine and
Water Streets, in New York, where the marriage ceremony
took place; President Smith, from the College at Princeton,
New Jersey, officiating on the occasion. From an autobiog-
raphy of her early life left by Mrs. Quincy, I copy an account
of the bridal journey to Boston, which reads strangely in
these days of steamboats and railroads: —

"We travelled pleasantly in a private carriage and four, and reached
Marlborough, Massachusetts, on the evening of the eighth day of our
journey. The next day, at noon, we saw a carriage approach, which
brought Mr. Quincy's mother, accompanied by his cousins, Miriam
Phillips and Hannah Storer, whom she had selected as appropriate
attendants on her new daughter. Mrs. Quincy was then fifty-three
years of age, still retaining traces of great personal beauty, with a fine
expression of countenance, and cordial and graceful manners. Her
dress united richness and elegance with propriety and taste. I was
much agitated at the thought of this meeting; but, from the moment I
saw her, and received her first welcome and embrace, I felt at ease,
and sure that we should promote each other's happiness. Mr. Quincy's
satisfaction was complete when he beheld me with his mother, and
surrounded by approving friends. The next day, we had a very gay
journey to Boston in the carriage with Mrs. Quincy and her com-

* This extract is from an interesting and valuable memoir of Mr. Quincy, which
appeared in the "New-York Daily Tribune" for July 8, 1864, a little more than a week
after his death. It is understood to have been written by his son, Mr. Edmund Quincy;
and the reader will find that we are under repeated obligations to it. Through the
kindness of the family, we have also had access to letters and other manuscripts, which
have been of great use in preparing this biographical notice.

panions, sending our luggage by the one which had brought us from New York. We drove over Cambridge Bridge, and through Boston, to the residence of Mrs. Quincy, in Pearl Street, where she again welcomed us to her home."

A happier matrimonial connection could not have been formed. By her delicacy of character, calm judgment, and literary culture, Mrs. Quincy was admirably qualified to preside over her husband's house with grace and dignity, and at the same time to enter into and share his best thoughts, and be his companion and adviser in all things. But their bright prospects, after a few short months, were suddenly clouded by the sickness and death of Mr. Quincy's mother. The event was unexpected, and widely deplored; yet all felt it to be a natural and impressive termination of the great purpose of her life, which was to bring up her son to be worthy of his name, and see him established in the world. Her work was done.*

In 1798, Mr. Quincy delivered the oration on the anniversary of American Independence, before the citizens of Boston. This is the first of his acknowledged productions which have been transmitted to us by the press. It is also, both in matter and manner, a characteristic performance, and seems to have attracted considerable attention at the time; for the copy now before us is a Philadelphia reprint of the Boston edition. The orator begins by recounting the principal causes which endangered the liberties of the Colonies; and then shows, or undertakes to show, that similar causes were still at work, under other names and connections, threatening the liberties of the United States. It was no longer England and her emissaries, but France and her emissaries. "The black whirlwind, which spreads disorder and desolation over the face of Europe, curls threatening towards our shores." In

---

* In the "Columbian Centinel" for March 28, 1798, there is an obituary notice of this lady, from the pen of Dr. Kirkland.

one word, it is an earnest and fearless statement of the imminent perils of the country, as apprehended at that time,
from the Federal point of view.

At the election for members of Congress, in 1800, Mr.
Quincy was the Federal candidate in the Suffolk district.
He was then but twenty-eight; at a time, too, when years
weighed much more than they do now as a qualification for
office. And besides, party lines, at least with the mass of
the people, were not yet so distinctly drawn as afterwards;
a circumstance which enabled the supporters of the rival
candidate, Dr. William Eustis, to urge with greater effect
his larger experience and his Revolutionary services. Dr.
Eustis was chosen by a small majority. In April, 1804, Mr.
Quincy was elected a member of the Massachusetts Senate,
and took an active part in the business of that body during
its summer session. But in the following November, before
his term of service there had expired, he was again put in
competition with Dr. Eustis for the office of representative
in Congress. This time his friends prevailed by a decided
vote, as they also did at his three successive re-elections;
after which he voluntarily retired, partly for political, and
partly for domestic and personal reasons.

In reviewing Mr. Quincy's Congressional career, every one
must be impressed by the vigor, intelligence, and inflexible
constancy with which he maintained what he conceived to be
the vital interests of the country. Reference is often made
to a few vehement expressions and acts of his, provoked by
the extreme measures of the day, as if they were a fair speci-
men of his public conduct; but this is not the case. Scarcely
a single question of importance came up for consideration by
Congress, during the eight years he was a member of that
body, on which he did not speak at length, discussing it on
its merits. His language is always terse and strong; his
information full and exact, showing how thoroughly he had
prepared himself for the work by a careful study of the his-

tory and resources of this country and its foreign relations,
of the dangers and safeguards of free governments, and of
international law. As a parliamentary orator, judged by his
printed speeches, he stands among the foremost this country
has produced. Where his only aim is to enlighten or con-
vince, the reasoning is often singularly compact and lucid;
as in his speech "on Fortifying the Coasts and Harbors," and
in that "on Establishing a Navy." Occasionally, as in what
he says of New England and his native State, in a speech "on
Submission to the Edicts of Great Britain and France," he
indulges in bursts of enthusiasm and flights of fancy, which
were much applauded at the time, and are still read with
pleasure. In bitter and scornful sarcasm he was unrivalled,
the consciousness of which tempted him to resort to this
mode of attack oftener, perhaps, than was well; but the debate "on the Influence of Place and Patronage" afforded him
ample and legitimate scope for it. It has been said of the
speech made by him on this occasion, that it ought to be
printed and glazed, and hung up in every office of every
office-holder in the land. John Adams, though dissenting
from several of its positions, pronounced "the eloquence mas-
terly, and the satire inimitable," unsurpassed by any thing in
Juvenal or Swift.

Mr. Quincy has been sometimes blamed for the violence of
his attacks on the Administration. This is one of those points
on which the party in power and the party out of power can
never be expected to agree. Even as a question of general
casuistry, it is not easy to settle, on purely ethical grounds,
precisely how far such opposition can be carried in great
national issues, and especially in time of war, without becoming factious or unpatriotic. When the Emperor Alexander
was in London, in 1814, he told one of the great Whig lords
that he liked the working of the Opposition Party, in England, on the whole; "but would it not be still better," he
asked, "if they were to communicate their objections to the

ministry *in private?*" Of course, Mr. Quincy entertained no
scruples of this kind; indeed, to a people accustomed to free
speech and a free press, the suggestion is simply ludicrous.
The only practical rule would seem to be, for every one to
expose and denounce what he conceives to be alarming public
abuses. If the abuses really exist, the people should know
it; if not, let the charge be refuted. To the objection that
the best governments may be weakened or obstructed by
such attacks, and this, too, in times of difficulty and peril,
when their energies are taxed to the utmost, the answer is
obvious. Where the people are used to unrestrained party
recrimination, they soon learn how to understand it, and
make the proper allowances; nay, more, if unreasonable or
ill-timed, it is much more likely to injure the party from
which it proceeds, than the party against which it is directed. And, besides, even if some inconvenience is occasioned thereby, it must be accepted as a necessary condition
of liberty; or, at any rate, as part of the price usually paid
for it.

Never, in the history of this country, has the Opposition
felt called upon to speak out more boldly than at the time
when Mr. Quincy was in Congress. The old leaders of the
Federal party had taken an active part in laying the foundations of the existing Government; they had also been among
the steady supporters of Washington's policy. It has sometimes been said, that they were the friends of *order*, rather
than of *liberty;* but there is not much ground for this distinction. They had just seen the wild and impracticable
notions of liberty prevalent in France end in a remorseless
military despotism; and, to their excited imaginations, things
in this country were rapidly drifting in the same direction.
Liberty, as well as order, at least to their apprehension, was
in imminent danger; but what could they do to save either?
Reduced to an inconsiderable minority in the national and
most of the State governments, neither their counsels nor

their votes were of any avail; leaving them no power but that of protest, pushed to the verge of resistance.

Whoever is familiar with the newspapers and political pamphlets of that day, will not need to be informed, that Mr. Quincy, in his most solemn warnings and vehement denunciations, seldom, if ever, went beyond the party he represented. Indeed, there were questions on which he did not go so far. In 1808, he voted with the majority on the resolution, "that the United States cannot, without a sacrifice of their rights, honor, and independence, submit to the edicts of Great Britain and France;" and, in 1811, on the bill for augmenting the land forces. Again, in 1812, he not only voted for the Government measure "to establish a navy," but made one of his ablest speeches in its favor. He also professed his readiness at all times to intrust the Executive with abundant means for putting the country in a state of defence. Moreover, injustice has often been done to the Federal Opposition in Congress, by inferring its general character from single and extreme acts; in proof of which it would be easy to adduce testimony not to be suspected of partiality. A single instance will suffice. The debate on the short Embargo immediately preceding the declaration of war against Great Britain had been continued until seven o'clock in the evening, and the Administration was anxious to hurry the bill through. In this state of things, Mr. Quincy expressed a desire to speak on the question, so extremely interesting to his immediate constituents, but was unable to do so from fatigue, unless the House would consent to an adjournment. An adjournment was therefore advocated by Mr. Williams, of South Carolina, and Mr. Macon, of North Carolina, both of them leading Democrats; the former assigning as a reason for the indulgence, that "the deportment of the other side of the House had, during the whole of the session, been very gentlemanly towards the majority." Mr. Macon went farther still: "He thought the minority had acted with more propriety than he ever knew in a minority." Even Mr. Wright, of Maryland, though opposed to the adjournment, " was willing to acknowledge the minority had conducted with propriety."

But occasionally there were stormy times. The following is an extract from a letter from Washington, dated Jan. 20, 1809 : * —

"Yesterday and to-day there has been in the House of Representatives one of the warmest and most impassioned discussions ever witnessed by a legislative assembly, on the bill for the next meeting of Congress. Mr. Quincy made an attack on the Administration, which called forth all the virulence of the Executive phalanx ; and, to-day, Campbell and Jackson went into the House, with the apparent determination to reduce him to the same necessity to which Gardenier was forced last session. Irritated by his attacks, and unable to answer him, they poured out upon him a torrent of gross and illiberal abuse. Mr. Quincy, in reply, stated specifically his ground, and told them that his honor was of little worth if it lay in the mouths of *such* men, and not in his own conduct. He was no *duellist.* He had the honor to represent, not only a wise, a moral, a powerful and intellectual, but a religious people ; that, among them, to avenge wrongs of words, by resorting to the course of conduct to which it was obviously intended to reduce him, was so far from being honorable, that it would be a disgrace to any man. To gain the temporary applause of such men as his assailants, whom he could only pity and despise, he should not sacrifice his own principles, nor forfeit the respect of those whose good opinion was the highest reward of his life. If they expected by such artifices to deter him from doing his duty, they would find themselves mistaken. Where *he was known*, nothing they could say would *injure him ;* and where *they were known*, he believed the effect would *not be greater.*"

Brought up in New England, and professing to be a man of moral and religious principle, he could, of course, take no other ground than he did on the subject of duelling ; but his open and manly way of avowing it won general admiration. Mr. Buckminster did but utter the common sentiment, when

---

* First published in the "New England Palladium," Jan. 31, 1809.

he said "he would rather be the author of that retort of his, than of all the speeches he ever made, however eloquent or effective." He also had another motive for being thus explicit. Only a fortnight before, his friends in Boston and Quincy had been startled by a rumor, which, from the difficulty of communication at that time, remained uncontradicted for several days, that he had actually fallen in an affair of honor, so called. He was glad of an opportunity to set their minds at rest on that point. As, however, some fears were entertained of an attack in the streets, Mr. Lloyd insisted on arming him with a brace of pistols, carefully loaded by himself, which he consented to wear for a few days, and then threw aside. He probably was never in any real danger; there was something in his look and bearing which did not encourage an assault. And, besides, it is interesting to know, that much of the indignation expressed against him on the floor of Congress did not grow out of personal or even party hostility, but was merely for political effect at home. One of the Western members was frank enough to tell him, that he was hated in his district more than any other man in the country, except perhaps Colonel Pickering. "So," says he, "I must go on abusing you, or I shall lose my next election. But I hope we shall be good friends notwithstanding."

How little he cared for such things appears from the fact, that, within a week after the scene just described, he gave occasion to another of the same kind. The latter, indeed, as the story is commonly told, would seem to have been little better than an act of Quixotism on his part; but it is because the circumstances which led to it, and his real objects, are kept out of sight: —

"The facts," as his son tells us,. "were these. General Lincoln, of the Revolution, was appointed Collector of Boston, by President Washington, and held the office down to 1809. His infirmities of age and health, however, had made him desirous of resigning his post; and in November, 1806, he had sent in his resignation [or wish to resign].

Mr. Jefferson asked him, as a personal favor, to retain the place until the next March. To this he consented, but in March no successor was appointed; and, after waiting till September, he again requested to be relieved, stating his entire inability to perform the duties of his office. To this communication he never received any answer at all; and he was compelled to remain in office, although he had not been able to be in Boston for nearly a year. This office had thus been kept virtually vacant for more than two years, as a provision for General Henry Dearborn, Mr. Jefferson's Secretary of War, after his term of office should have expired." *

To Mr. Quincy's strict notions of public duty, this sort of favoritism in the bestowment of Executive patronage, involving, as it did in the present instance, the retention in an important office for so long a time of a person known to be wholly incompetent to its duties, amounted to "a high misdemeanor," deserving the notice and action of Congress. Nor was this all. While he was meditating what to do, an article appeared in the "National Intelligencer," the organ of the Government, stigmatizing General Lincoln as "a Federalist, whom *the forbearance of the Administration* had long retained in office, in opposition to the wishes of a respectable class in the community." Incensed at the false impression which such a statement was calculated to make on the public mind, Mr. Quincy was determined that the whole truth should be known. Accordingly, he rose in his place in the House on that very morning, as soon as the business of the day began,

---

* These facts are given more at length, in a letter to Mr. Quincy from Benjamin Weld, Esq., Assistant-Collector of Boston, dated Jan. 19, 1809. The writer says, "Early in the month of November, 1806, General Lincoln wrote to the President of the United States, stating his infirmities and advanced years, and requested to resign at the end of the year. The President returned an answer which was received in December, which, after some flattering compliments on his Revolutionary services, requested the General to give him a little longer time to look out for a suitable character to fill his office, and limited the time to the last of March following, beyond which, he *assured* him, he should not be *detained.* The General in reply said, 'The wishes of the President should be a law to him.'" General Lincoln's request was afterwards urgently renewed; but no attention whatever was paid to it for nearly two years. Mr. Weld says, "That the office has been kept for General D., there is not the least doubt; he has intimated it himself to persons who have told me in confidence."

and, after stating the facts he was prepared to prove, moved the two following resolutions: First, that the President be requested to communicate the correspondence respecting General Lincoln's resignation; and, secondly, that a Committee be appointed to inquire into the causes which have prevented that resignation from being accepted, and report the result. A violent debate ensued, and, when the vote was taken on the question, "Shall the Resolutions be adopted?" it stood, yeas, 1; nays, 117.

In looking back on this affair, we need not suppose that Mr. Quincy submitted his motion in the expectation that it would lead to an *impeachment*, or even so much as bring up the question in that form. Before the vote was taken, his main purpose had been accomplished, which was to expose the conduct of the President. Having done this, it would have been in order for him to withdraw his motion; but, as such a step might be construed into a shrinking from responsibility, he chose rather to let it take its course. Characteristically enough, he told the House, that "neither the asperities of his political opponents, nor the disagreement of his political friends, would change his mind on a subject which he had well considered. If he was in an error concerning the charge, or rather allegation, he had made, he was willing to stand before the nation in support of it. It gave him no sort of pain or anxiety." The motion was made at the opening of the morning's session, which then began at nine o'clock. At twelve o'clock the same day, General Dearborn's nomination was sent to the Senate.*

---

* Mr. Randall, in his "Life of Thomas Jefferson," vol. iii. p. 289, dwells on the Revolutionary services of General Lincoln. But it was not for these that he was detained in office against his will by Mr Jefferson. Again, he says, it was no "hardship" to be complained of on the part of the General or his friends, that he continued to receive a salary of five thousand dollars a year for doing nothing. Perhaps not; but, nevertheless, it might be connected with an abuse of Executive patronage; and, besides, the responsibility under the circumstances was felt and declared to be a "hardship." Finally, he says of Lincoln's resignation, that it was "never actually sent in

There was also another passage in Mr. Quincy's Congressional life which deserves notice, because it has been made the ground of representing him as the first asserter in the National legislature of the right of secession. It occurred Jan. 14, 1811, in the debate on "admitting the Territory of Orleans into the Union as an Independent State." In a constitutional argument on that question, he was led to say : —

"'I am compelled to declare it as my deliberate opinion, that, if this bill passes, the bonds of this Union are virtually dissolved ; that the States which compose it are free from their moral obligations ; and that as it will be the right of all, so it will be the duty of some, to prepare definitely for a separation, — amicably if they can, violently if they must.'

"Mr. Quincy was here called to order by Mr. Poindexter.

"Mr. Quincy repeated and justified the remark he had made, which, to save all misapprehension, he committed to writing in the following words : 'If this bill passes, it is my deliberate opinion that it is virtually a dissolution of this Union ; that it will free the States from their moral obligation ; and as it will be the right of all, so it will be the duty of some, definitely to prepare for a separation, amicably if they can, violently if they must.'

"After some confusion, Mr. Poindexter required the decision of the Speaker, whether it was consistent with the propriety of debate, to use such an expression. He said it was radically wrong for any member to use arguments going to dissolve the Government, and tumble this body itself to dust and ashes. It would be found, from the gentleman's statement of his language, that he had declared the right of any portion of the people to separate —

"Mr. Quincy wished the Speaker to decide ; for, if the gentleman was permitted to debate the question, he should lose one-half of his speech.

"The Speaker decided, that great latitude in debate was generally

---

until after the passage of the Enforcing Law," which took place about a fortnight only before the appointment of Dearborn. The statement is, perhaps, true so far as this, that Lincoln from courtesy contented himself with pressing his request, and allowed himself to be put off until the passage of that Act. He is then understood to have written to the President, "that he had fought for the liberties of his country, and spent his best years in her service; and that he was not, in his old age, to be made an instrument to violate what he had assisted to acquire."

allowed; and that, by way of argument against the bill, the first part of the gentleman's observations was admissible; but the latter member of the sentence, viz., 'That it would be the duty of some States to prepare for a separation, amicably if they can, violently if they must,' was contrary to the order of debate.

"Mr. Quincy appealed from this decision, and required the yeas and nays on the appeal. The question was thus stated: 'Is the decision of the Speaker correct?' And decided, fifty-three yeas; fifty-six nays. So the decision of the Speaker was reversed; Mr. Quincy's observations were declared to be in order, and he proceeded." *

Such is the record. The first reflection suggested by it is, that the House, though composed of political opponents in the proportion of two to one, pronounced his remarks "in order." No doubt many of them acted on the principle, that language elicited in the heat of an impassioned debate is not to be interpreted to the letter. Above all, the purpose, the drift of the speaker should be considered; which, in the present case, was not to threaten, but to warn; not a plot to destroy the Union, but anxiety to save it. On resuming his speech, Mr. Quincy said, "When I spoke of the separation of the States as resulting from the violation of the Constitution contemplated in this bill, I spoke of it as a necessity deeply to be deprecated; but as resulting from causes so certain and obvious, as to be absolutely inevitable, when the effect of the principle is practically experienced. It is to preserve, to guard the constitution of my country, that I denounce this attempt." — "The voice I have uttered, at which gentlemen startle with such agitation, is no unfriendly voice: I intend it as a voice of warning." †

_____

* Benton's Abridgment of the Debates of Congress, vol. iv. p. 327.

† His purpose and drift in this speech are made still more apparent from the following account of it, given at the time in a private letter to Mrs. Quincy: "I used strong language, because, by calling on the North to separate, I knew it would rouse the Southern men, who, though they are eternally throwing out threats of separation *themselves*, and thus govern the country with a rod of iron, yet tremble like aspen leaves at such a proposition coming from the North. I answered my purpose fully. The House were so arrested by my boldness, that they heard me throughout; and Poindexter has made my position so prominent, that I have no doubt the nation will do the

Precisely what he meant by releasing the old States from
" their *moral* obligations " to the Union, is not clear. If he
merely meant, that persistence in an *open* and *avowed* violation of the original terms of the compact on the part of the
Government would render that compact morally null and
void, the doctrine is incontestable. But, if the alleged violation here complained of was really open and avowed, that is
to say, acknowledged to be a violation on all sides, why go
into an elaborate argument, as he does, to prove what no-
body denied?* On the other hand, if the violation was
asserted by one party, and denied by the other, — this being
one of the principal questions at issue, as the debate shows,
— it certainly was not competent for any State, as such,
to decide the question for itself, and act accordingly. At
the same time it is proper to observe, that Mr. Quincy's
doctrine, however construed or judged, differs essentially,
both in nature and extent, from that out of which the great
Southern secession arose ; the latter being, that any State, by
virtue of its sovereignty alone, has a right to secede from
the Union for any cause deemed sufficient by itself, no matter
whether the Constitution has been violated or not.

---

same. If people in our part of the Union are tame on this question, which I deem
both in principle and consequences the most important ever debated, they deserve to
be, what they will be, *slaves*, and to no desirable masters."

* Mr. Jefferson, as a "strict constructionist," had, it is true, entertained scruples
on this subject at the time of the original purchase of Louisiana; but they were not
shared, certainly not to the same extent, by his party in Congress, — not even by
the Southern members. In this very debate, Mr. Macon, of North Carolina, admitted
that the constitutional objection, if well-founded, ought to prevail; and this, too, not-
withstanding any stipulations in the treaty of cession to the contrary. " It is never too
late," said he, " to return to the Constitution." Mr. Jefferson himself was induced at
length to acquiesce, consistently or inconsistently, in a more liberal interpretation of
that instrument on the point in question, — an interpretation, we may add, which has
since been acted on repeatedly without much opposition, though it has never come up
for adjudication in the Supreme Court. " At the present day," says Judge Story, " few
statesmen are to be found who seriously contest the constitutionality of the Acts
respecting either the Embargo, or the purchase and admission of Louisiana into the
Union. The general voice of the nation has sustained and supported them." (Com-
mentaries on the Constitution, vol. iii. p. 163.) — Perhaps such questions should be
regarded as *political* rather than as *juridical.*

But it was not in debate alone that Mr. Quincy evinced his zeal to serve his constituents. The representative of a large commercial district like Boston, besides his proper official charge in Congress, is expected to mediate between individuals and the Government in a multitude of difficulties and grievances incident to foreign traffic, and to keep a vigilant eye on the bearing of every new measure on their interests. This care, always onerous, was made doubly so at the time in question, by what has been called the anti-commercial policy of the Administration; but Mr. Quincy, to whom work throughout life was not so much a duty as a passion, neglected nothing. A single instance will illustrate his vigor and promptness. The dominant party having come to the conclusion, in the spring of 1812, to declare war against Great Britain, had made up their minds to impose an embargo of sixty days as a preliminary step: —

" Mr. Calhoun, on the eve of reporting this bill, communicated the purpose to Mr. Quincy, as the representative of a commercial district, in order that there might be no pretence of a surprise. Mr. Quincy at once advised with Mr. Lloyd, one of the Massachusetts senators, and instantly dispatched a special messenger to Boston with the intelligence. This courier accomplished the distance in what was then regarded as the incredibly short time of seventy-two hours. In consequence of this dispatch, great numbers of ships were loaded and sent to sea, neither the night nor the Sabbath interrupting the work of necessity, before the news arrived by the regular channels. Mr. Calhoun was not well pleased with this speedy advantage taken of his intelligence; but, as there was no particular purpose of pleasing him in the matter, it was of the less consequence." *

Mr. Quincy's fourth term of office as member of Congress expired in March, 1813. He had declined being considered a candidate for re-election, much to the regret of his political friends; but he could not be turned from his purpose. One

* Memoir in the New York Tribune.

reason was, that he had become weary of leading the forlorn
hope of Federalism in the national councils; and the more so,
as Federalism was beginning to be a house divided against
itself. He was also influenced, in no small measure, by domestic considerations. For three winters he had taken his family
with him to Washington; but this course, as the family increased, was attended by difficulty and expense he was
unwilling to incur. He was therefore under the necessity
of being separated from his wife and children for a considerable portion of every year; a great sacrifice to a man of his
tastes and habits, and one which he did not feel called upon
to make any longer, especially as he now saw that the most
strenuous opposition to democratic measures, in the existing
state of parties, would be of no avail.*

In thus withdrawing from Congress, at least until better
times, it was no part of Mr. Quincy's plan to retire from
public life. He was immediately elected by substantially the
same constituency to his former place in the Senate of Massachusetts, and continued an active and influential member of
that body for seven years, from 1813 to 1820. Here he acted
with the majority, and took his full share of the responsibility
in moulding and determining the policy of this State during
the last war with England.

Early in the June session of 1813, he was appointed chair-
man of a Committee to consider the recent formation of " new
States without the territorial limits of the United States."
His report is a restatement of the doctrine advanced in his
Congressional speeches on this subject, though under a some-
what mitigated form. The measure is denounced, not as

---

* The vexation and despondency which had already taken possession of some of
the best minds in the Federal party, may be judged of by the following passage, taken
from a letter of Fisher Ames to Mr. Quincy, while the latter was in Congress: "I declare to you, I fear Federalism will not only die, but all remembrance of it be lost. As
a party, it is still good for every thing it ever was good for; that is to say, to cry ' fire '
and ' stop thief,' when Jacobinism attempts to burn and rob. It never had the power
to put out the fire, or to seize the thief." — *Works of Fisher Ames*, vol. i. p. 301.

justifying, but as "tending to the dissolution of the Confederacy."

A few days afterwards, it was proposed to the Senate to pass certain resolves, in commendation of the gallantry and good conduct of Captain Lawrence, in the capture of a British brig of war. Similar resolves had been passed by both branches of the Legislature, in favor of other naval commanders; they had also been passed by the House, in this particular case, by a unanimous vote. In the Senate, however, they were now met by the famous preamble and resolution submitted by Mr. Quincy, declaring among other things, "that in a war like the present, waged without justifiable cause and prosecuted in a manner which indicates that conquest and ambition are its real motives, it is not becoming a moral and religious people to express any approbation of military or naval exploits which are not immediately connected with the defence of the coast and the soil." The passage of this resolution was regarded at the time as a triumph of the "conscientious Federalists," so called; it never had the approval of many of the leading members of the party, especially among the Boston merchants, who doubted the wisdom of speaking in this way of the victories achieved by our arms, and who were also concerned about their own interests, and fond of making a distinction in favor of the navy over the land forces. In the Democratic journals, it was everywhere fiercely denounced as "moral treason."

The unequal burdens and hardships imposed on New England by the Embargo, and afterwards by the war, continued to bear more and more heavily on the people, and produced a wide-spread spirit of discontent. This effect was still further aggravated by a suspicion, well or ill founded, that the South and West were in a conspiracy to cripple and destroy commerce, on which New England mainly depended for its wealth and prosperity, and to introduce Mr. Jefferson's "Chinese" policy. Under these circumstances the Hartford Convention

assembled, in 1814; not (as we believe is now generally
conceded) to increase or give effect to the disaffection, but
to control it and keep it within constitutional limits. Mr.
Quincy's relations to the whole movement are thus indicated
by his son : —

"When the Legislature of Massachusetts came to appoint delegates,
they omitted to elect Mr. Quincy. They were afraid to trust his im-
petuous temperament and fiery earnestness. They thought that he
would represent too well the spirit of those who demanded the Convention. He always described the Convention as 'a Tub to the
Whale,' as a dilatory measure to amuse the malcontents and make them
believe that something was doing for their relief, and keep them quiet
under inaction, until events might make action necessary. And this
did actually happen. One day, while the public attention was fixed
upon the Convention, then sitting with closed doors, a friend met Mr.
Quincy in the street, and said, 'What do you suppose will be the
result of this Convention?'—'I can tell you exactly,' he replied.
'Indeed,' exclaimed the other; 'pray what will it be?'—'A GREAT
PAMPHLET,' was his answer; and it was even so."

But it would be doing great injustice to Mr. Quincy to
suppose, that his thoughts, as a legislator, were wholly or
mainly occupied on questions of party politics. He was
ever ready with his earnest and effective support of well-
considered schemes for reform in prison discipline and in the
poor-laws, for the relief of insolvent debtors, for the encour-
agement of agriculture and popular education, and, in short,
for all philanthropic measures. Indeed, it was his independent course in respect to some of these measures, as well as the
stand he took in 1819, with a small minority composed mostly
of Democrats, against the separation of the District of Maine,*

---

* The first bill passed by the Legislature on this subject, in 1816, was not accepted
by the people of Maine. When the second, which really went into effect, was under
consideration, in 1819, Mr. Quincy resisted it strenuously in an eloquent and characteristic speech of two hours, in which he says: "Three years since, when a bill containing
similar provisions to that which is now on the table was passed, it was my misfortune
to be compelled to give it at this Board my *solitary* negative." He still stood alone in
the Committee, a circumstance which he thus notices: "I call this situation of mine a

which had the effect seriously to compromise his popularity with the managers of his own party. The consequence was, that, in making up the ticket for senators, in 1820, his name was dropped.* His personal and many of his political friends were offended at this step; and, being determined that the public should not lose his services, they succeeded in getting him elected to the House. Soon after taking his seat in that body, Mr. Mills, the Speaker, resigned, and he was called to the chair, — a place which he continued to hold until January, 1822, when he also resigned, in order to accept the appointment of Judge of the Municipal Court, in Boston.

Mr. Quincy's political life may be said to have now closed. This is the less to be regretted, inasmuch as the Federal party, the only party to which he ever properly belonged, was fast breaking up. The Federalists had never entirely

misfortune; for, if I know myself, I am not ambitious of that sort of distinction which arises from mere singularity, either in conduct or opinion. I have accordingly, and sedulously too, endeavored to raise a doubt upon this question; but I cannot. I could as well doubt of my own existence as doubt of the unconstitutionality of this bill. And, on an occasion of such magnitude and solemnity, he who cannot doubt, cannot compromise." When the final question was taken in the Senate, the votes were, — yeas, 26; nays, 11.

* A communication to the "Boston Daily Advertiser" for April 18, 1820, understood to be from Mr. John Lowell, throws light on this transaction. "Why," the writer asks, "are the county of Suffolk and the State deprived of the experience and talents of Mr. Quincy? To him the result will probably be beneficial, since it has given him an opportunity, most honorable to his character, of showing his magnanimity and disinterestedness. I would rather enjoy the triumph which that gentleman won at the late Federal caucus, than to have the unanimous suffrages of a fickle and ungrateful party. No: I will not say party, because I believe that at least three-quarters of the Federal party, left to their unbiassed suffrages, not alarmed by reports that Mr. Quincy would not be supported, and that, of course, their exertions to secure his election would be in vain, would have given them their unqualified and zealous support. The fault I find with this issue is, that it seems to hold out to the world an opinion that something more than uncorrupted integrity, unquestionable purity of manners and character, cultivated understanding, long experience in public affairs, and an ardent zeal to promote the honor and interests of the country, and the cause of religion and science, is expected of our rulers. And what is this something more that we expect? Is it a time-serving spirit and flattering manners? Is it dereliction of principle to preserve one's popularity? I repeat it, I would rather be Josiah Quincy, urging in a private assembly his fellow-citizens to do their duty, and to unite in favor of a list from which his own name was ungratefully excluded, than to have had the unanimous applause of both parties."

recovered from their misunderstanding with John Adams,
and still less from the defection of his son; but the actual
dissolution of the party, at least as a national one, is commonly dated from the so-called "era of good feelings," introduced at the inauguration of President Monroe, in 1817.
So rapid and complete was this dissolution, that, on the reconstruction of parties at the election of John Quincy Adams to
the Presidency, in 1824, nothing was left of Federalism,—not
even the name. Few if any instances are on record of a
party of equal merit and renown passing away so suddenly
and so entirely. It has been succeeded in Massachusetts by
parties of various denominations, some of which must have
found difficulty in telling what they *were;* but all knew what
they were *not,*— they were *not* Federalists. To the last,
however, Mr. Quincy was "faithful found among the faith-
less;" yet with a clear understanding that the old party could
never be revived. In reply to a letter written to him in
1847, on the subject of a "History of Federalism," he says:—

"It is not, however, to be concealed, that there is now no such thing
possible as the return of such influences. The circumstances of our
country no longer permit any such purity of motives, as characterized
the Federal policy, to be either a general or an efficient principle of
party action. The Federal leaders had a clear stage. They were not
embarrassed by precedents or examples. They had a homogeneous
population to guide, not a composite of all nations and languages. They
had for the basis of their power the character and influences of Washington, whose virtues, tried through the War of the Revolution, gave a
weight and secured a popularity for their measures, which no future
combination of men can hope to attain or possess. . . . The principles of Federalism lasted in power but twelve years, and in purity can
never be restored to it. *Opposuit Natura.*"

Seventeen of the best years of Mr. Quincy's life had been
given to legislation and statesmanship. Before passing to
other topics, it may be well to consider how far his political
theories have been confirmed by events.

These theories, as entertained at that time, are best expressed in his "Oration before the Washington Benevolent
Society," delivered by him in 1813, soon after his retirement
from Congress. According to him, the principal danger to
be apprehended in this country was from the disturbance of
"the proportions of political power," occasioned "partly by
the operation of the slave-ratio in the Constitution, and partly
by the unexampled emigration into the West." As a natural
consequence, the preponderance of the old States would be
gradually transferred to the new; and, what is worse, a new
national policy would be established favorable to the agricultural States, and adverse to the commercial States. New
England must, perhaps, submit to this up to a certain point,
as "the fair result of *the compact.*"

"We had agreed," says he, "that all the people within the ancient
limits of the United States should be placed on the same footing, and
had granted an undoubted right to Congress to admit States at will,
within the ancient limits. We had done more; we had submitted to
throw our rights and liberties, and those of our children, into a common stock with the Southern men and their slaves, and had agreed
to be content with what remained after they and their negroes were
served."

But the admission of Louisiana into the Union, deemed by
him clearly unconstitutional, had put a new face on the whole
transaction. Our allegiance to "a certain extrinsic associa-
tion called the United States" is limited by the condition,
that "the principles of the Constitution should be preserved
inviolate." — "Whether any such violation has occurred, or
whether it be such as essentially affects the securities of their
rights and liberties, are questions which the people of the
associated States are competent, not only to discuss, but *to
decide.*" His conclusion is, that "the people of this country
have but two events between which to select, and that at no
distant period of time: either to put an end to this oppres-
sion, and the chance of its recurrence, by a new and amicable

modification of the proportions and powers of the Constitution; or to worry along a little farther, until the weight of grievances produce convulsions which will put an end to the Constitution." *

Time has sanctioned some of these speculations, and set aside others. He was certainly among the first to see, in all its extent, the danger to be apprehended from the slaveholding power. Occupied almost exclusively with the political aspects of slavery, there was no man in those early days so profoundly impressed by the conviction, that out of that institution would grow jealousies and contentions which would shake the Union to its foundations. So far, he is to be reckoned among the prophets. But in other respects his forebodings, or many of them at least, though shared by some of the best and wisest men of his party, have not been fulfilled. New England, by adding manufactures to commerce, and bringing to both the exhaustless resources of free and skilled labor, has never ceased to prosper under the Constitution as it was, and as it is. Again, he did not make sufficient account of the many ties of interest and sympathy

---

* There can be no doubt that the views here advanced were generally entertained by the party, not excepting its Southern members. Alexander C. Hanson, of Baltimore, wrote: "You mistake the feelings and wishes of the Federalists with whom I communicate, if you suppose the language of your oration too strong, or your suggestions offensive. Our only fear was, that the leading men of Massachusetts would lack boldness. We groan and sweat under domestic tyranny, as much as our brethren in the New-England States; we turn an anxious eye on your proceedings, and receive your speech as a pledge of actions suitable to such language. Our only chance for relief and salvation depends on the vigor and intrepidity of the New-England States. There is a short and sure road to relief; and, sooner or later, it must be taken. The South and West will continue to govern us as long as the North and East are willing to be governed."

What John Randolph, who belonged to no party, thought of this oration, is thus expressed to one of his correspondents: "Mr. Quincy sent me a copy of his speech of the 30th of last month. It is a composition of much ability and depth of thought; but it indicates a spirit and a temper to the North which is more a subject of regret than of surprise. The grievances of Lord North's administration were but a feather in the scale, when compared with those inflicted by Jefferson and Madison." (Garland's "Life of John Randolph.") — Mr. Quincy is said to have been almost the only friend of Randolph with whom he never quarrelled.

between the free Atlantic States and the free inland States, new as well as old, which, in a great national struggle, were almost sure to enlist them on the same side. Neither could he foresee that vast network of railroad communication which is now doing so much to bind together the East and the West, and secure the prosperity of both.

Moreover, the theory of the Constitution advanced by him in Congress, and re-affirmed, as we understand it, in this oration, is not that which is now generally held, at least by loyal men. How can any State or section of States proceed " to discuss and decide " the perilous question, whether the Constitution has been violated, or not, without usurping the authority which that very Constitution has expressly delegated to the Supreme Court? So that, even if the Constitution were to be regarded as a simple and ordinary "compact," dependent for its obligation on the continued fulfilment of all its conditions, the right contended for could not be sustained. In point of fact, however, according to the highest authority on this subject, the Constitution, in strictness of language, is not *a compact* at all, but *a government founded on a compact,* — a government thenceforth resting on its own power to enforce its own will. " When the people agree to erect a government, and actually erect it, the thing is done, and the agreement is at an end. The compact is executed, and the end designed by it attained." * On this doctrine, and, as it would seem, on this doctrine alone, can a coerced Union, or a Union restored by force, be reconciled with republican principles or the right of self-government.

At the same time, the enlightened and candid historian, in pronouncing judgment on the positions taken by the Federalists at the period now under consideration, will make large allowance for the difference between the circumstances under which they lived and thought, and those under which we live and think. It has been said of Tycho Brahe, that, *with the evidence as it then stood*, he was right in maintaining his false theory of the heavens against the true one of Copernicus. A similar remark is applicable to the leaders of Federalism at the time of which we are now speaking. The evidence, as it then stood, was often on their side, when the truth was not. Even in those respects in which their apprehensions or their policy have been overruled and set aside by experience, it has been by the experience which followed, and not by that which went before. Accordingly, it may be said, that, when the old Federalists were wrong and the old Democrats right, it was, in many cases at least, because the former looked to reason and precedent, while the latter trusted in their feelings and instincts. How, indeed, was it possible for men acting year after year in a hopeless and continually decreasing minority, every new measure of public importance seeming to them a downward step, their imaginations haunted, meanwhile, by the excesses and issues of the French Revolution, — how was it possible for such men, so circumstanced, not to lose more or less of their confidence in the stability of the existing Government, and in the popular will? Happily, however, Mr. Quincy lived to have his faith in both abundantly restored, and to see and acknowledge, even in those events which most perplexed him at the time, the hand of God.

The appointment of Mr. Quincy to the bench of the Municipal Court, in 1822, after he had been withdrawn from the practice of his profession for nearly twenty years, occasioned some surprise. But without much reason; for the jurisdiction of this court was exclusively criminal, and he was known never to have remitted his attention to the best means of dealing with the suffering and dangerous classes, or to the changes made or contemplated in the criminal law.

He retained this place but little more than a year; yet one of his decisions has permanently connected his name with

the history of Law Reform. It was in the action against Mr.
Buckingham, editor of the "New-England Galaxy," for a libel
on J. N. Maffitt, a noted preacher of that day, which came up
for trial in the December Term of 1822. The prosecuting officer in this case had agreed to waive an advantage understood
to be given him by the law as it then was, and to allow the
defendant to prove the truth in evidence. But the Judge
objected to this course, on the ground that, if the law of
Massachusetts really and purposely excluded such testimony,
the Court was not at liberty to permit its introduction merely
on the plea of an agreement of parties. He then went into
a full discussion of the legal point at issue, undertaking to
deduce, from the Constitutional guaranty of a free press in
this Commonwealth, that every one here has the right to
publish the truth from good motives; and hence the admissi-
bility of the truth in evidence in all cases of prosecution for
libel, — not, indeed, as being a justification in all cases, but as
bearing essentially on the question of motive or intent to be
decided by the jury.

Objections were made at the time to both the substance
and form of this ruling of the Judge; and it does not appear
to have been generally accepted as law.* In the very same
court, when Mr. Buckingham was arraigned before it again
for libel, in 1824, he was not allowed to prove the truth of

---

* The decision was not only commented on in the newspapers, but called forth two
considerable pamphlets. The first was "A Letter to the Hon. Josiah Quincy, Judge of
the Municipal Court in the City of Boston, on the Law of Libel, as laid down by him
in the Case of Commonwealth v. Buckingham. By a Member of the Suffolk Bar."
It contests many of his positions, taking substantially the old "common-law" ground,
that the sole object of public prosecutions for libel is to prevent breaches of the peace;
and that, viewed in this light, the truth or falsehood of the statement is immaterial, —
nay, that the truth of the statement often aggravates the evil. It was soon followed by
"Reflections upon the Law of Libel, in a Letter addressed to a Member of the Suffolk
Bar. By a Citizen;" in which the other side is argued with ability and discrimination,
and the personalities in the "Letter" are successfully and indignantly repelled. Both
of the pamphlets were published anonymously, the author of the "Letter" not being
known or suspected at the time by the author of the "Reflections." Afterwards, it was
under stood that the former was Harrison Gray Otis, jun., and the latter, Edmund
Kimball, then young lawyers in Boston.

the publication, though it was asked for expressly, not as a
justification, but to rebut the charge of malice. Still we are
not to suppose that Mr. Quincy's courageous defence of a free
press was without effect. There is every reason to believe,
that his forcible statement of what the law *ought to be*, together with the discussion to which it gave rise, had great
weight in determining the Legislature of Massachusetts to
pass an Act in 1827, granting, in express terms, to the defendant in prosecutions for libel, the very right which he had
contended for on the ground of the common law controlled
by the Constitution of the State. However this may be, it is
certain that a law of libel, substantially the same with that
laid down by Judge Quincy, has since been adopted in every
State in the Union, either by statute, or by express provision
of the Constitution. And the same is also true of England;
in short, wherever the press is unshackled, that is to say,
wherever men are allowed to publish *the truth*, with good
motives and for justifiable ends, whether in respect to "public
characters" or private citizens.

After serving his native city for fifteen months on the
bench, Mr. Quincy accepted the more difficult and responsible
office of its chief magistrate, which he held nearly six years.
Boston owes much to the circumstance, that its most distinguished citizens, men born and brought up there, and for this
reason feeling a natural and just pride in its institutions and
good name, have always been willing to take an active part
in municipal affairs. The Revolutionary renown associated
with the old town organization and the old name, together
with a strong democratic fondness for transacting public business in popular assemblies, induced the inhabitants to reject
several attempts to introduce a city government from as far
back as 1784. At length, however, in 1821, the population
had grown to be so large as to make the old system manifestly
inadequate; and a city charter was therefore obtained and
finally adopted, though not without strenuous resistance in

which Mr. Quincy participated to some extent.* Still, not-withstanding this opposition, when the canvass was opened for the first Mayor, he was put forward as a prominent candi-date, and actually received the largest number of votes at the first trial. But no choice being made, and serious political misunderstandings having arisen, he immediately withdrew his name, as did also the other candidates; † and at the next trial Mr. John Phillips was elected by a union of all parties. Mr. Phillips retired at the end of the year, and was suc-ceeded by Mr. Quincy, who was inducted into office with the usual forms, May 1, 1823.

In the short administration of his predecessor, little had been attempted, except to organize the new form of govern-ment, and put it in working order. All the great reforms so confidently anticipated from the change were still to be effected; a work which could not have fallen into more faith-ful and resolute hands.

One of Mr. Quincy's first objects was to carry into full effect a scheme commenced two years before, by a committee appointed by the town, of which he was chairman. Even at

---

* Mr. Quincy is said, in the Memoir by his son, to have "strongly opposed this change, thinking that the old system of town government was the best adapted to the habits and wants of the citizens, and the least liable to abuses." Also, when he was first nominated for Mayor, it was objected, that he had been "the most zealous and active opponent of the city charter." That he was opposed to some parts of the new scheme and of the proposed charter, there can be no doubt; but that he wished to retain "the old system," is hardly consistent with what he says in his "Municipal History of Boston." He there tells us (p. 28), that "the impracticability of conduct-ing the municipal interests of the place under the form of Town Government" had become "apparent to the inhabitants." With seven thousand qualified voters convened in town-meeting, it was, as he goes on to show, "evidently impossible calmly to de-liberate and act;" and, in consequence, "a few busy or interested individuals easily obtained the management of the most important affairs."

† The other candidates were the Hon. Harrison Gray Otis, and the Hon. Thomas L. Winthrop. The following is Mr. Quincy's account of this political *imbroglio:* "When I promised a body of my fellow-citizens to stand, Otis was not in the field; he was a member of the United-States Senate, and his intention to run for the mayoralty was un-known to me. When informed he was a candidate, I solicited the Committee to whom my promise had been made to release me from it, as I had no wish to run against Mr. Otis; but they refused."

that time, the abuses connected with the almshouse in Leverett Street had aroused public attention to the necessity of
some change in the care of the poor, and of making some
distinction between the virtuous and the vicious poor. In
pursuance of this end, the committee just mentioned had already purchased above sixty acres of land in South Boston,
and erected upon it a House of Industry; in order that the
able-bodied among its inmates might find, in cultivating the
ground, what was believed to be the most healthful, and at
the same time the most profitable, employment. But the
whole plan was in danger of being frustrated by a multitude
of obstacles, growing partly out of lingering prejudices against
the workhouse system, and partly out of the jealousy of offi-
cials and the disputed jurisdiction of rival Boards, which it
required all Mr. Quincy's courage and determination to overcome. Even with his utmost exertions, it was not until April,
1825, that the last occupants of the almshouse were transferred to South Boston. Meanwhile, a House of Correction
had been built there under the same auspices; and this was
soon followed by the House of Reformation for Juvenile
Offenders. There can be no doubt, that a large and growing
city would have found it necessary sooner or later to make
these or similar provisions. Still, it is to the credit of Mr.
Quincy that he hastened the measure, and by hastening it
was able to secure an eligible location for the experiment in
the neighborhood, before the opportunity was for ever lost.*

His attention was next called to the sanitary and police
regulations, which, from the remissness or timidity of the
authorities, had not kept pace with the growth of the city.
No part of the present arrangement for securing cleanliness,
comfort, and health, which is the just pride of the citizens,

---

* For the sixty-three acres, which constituted at first the City Farm in South Boston, only one hundred dollars an acre were given, though, before the signing of the
deed, five hundred dollars were offered the original proprietor. Land in that vicinity
soon afterwards rose to one thousand dollars an acre.

was then in operation. For introducing it, they are mainly indebted to Mr. Quincy; and some notion of the extent of the reform may be gathered from the fact, that, under the new system, more than three thousand tons of dirt and decaying substances of every kind, accumulated on the wharves and in the narrow streets and alleys, were removed in a single month. "For the first time, on any general scale destined for universal application, the *broom* was used upon the streets. On seeing this novel spectacle of files of sweepers, an old and common adage was often applied to the new administration of city affairs; in good humor by some, in a sarcastic spirit by others." *

Nor were his measures less prompt and decisive for suppressing social and moral nuisances; one instance of which will suffice to illustrate the character of the new *régime*. By a strange anomaly, in one of the most orderly and decorous cities in the world, another Alsatia, on a small scale, had been suffered to grow up in a part of what was then called West Boston, where the law, and the officers appointed to enforce it, were openly set at defiance.

"Twelve or fourteen houses of infamous character were openly kept, without concealment and without shame. The chief officer of the former police said to the Mayor, soon after his inauguration, 'There are dances there almost every night. The whole street is in a blaze of light from their windows. To put them down without a military force seems impossible: a man's life would not be safe who should attempt it. The company consists of highbinders, jail-birds, known thieves and miscreants, with women of the worst description. Murders, it is well known, have been committed there, and more have been

---

* Quincy's "Municipal History of Boston," p. 68. The bills of mortality afford a striking proof of the wisdom and effectiveness of these sanitary measures. For the ten years which preceded Mr. Quincy's accession to the mayoralty, in 1823, the annual average proportion of deaths to the population in Boston was about one to forty-two; during the next four years, it was less than one to fifty; and in the last three years of his administration, ending with 1828, it was but one to fifty-seven. — *Ibid*, p. 267. It is understood, that the usual average of mortality in cities of equal population was at that time about one to forty-seven.

suspected.' He was asked, 'if vice and villany were too strong for the police.' He replied, 'I think so; at least, it has long been so in that quarter.' He was answered, 'There shall be at least a struggle for the supremacy of the laws.'"*

In such a struggle, resolutely undertaken by Mr. Quincy, there could be no doubt about the issue. The whole district was put under ban; all licenses were revoked; a vigorous police was organized; and, before the expiration of Mr. Quincy's first official term, that section of the city was as quiet and safe as any other.†

But the most enduring monument of his services as Mayor is the Market-house which bears his name. At first, nothing more was contemplated than to extend the accommodations already afforded in the basement of Faneuil Hall. Even this, however, when brought up for consideration before a meeting of the citizens, was scouted by many as a wasteful extravagance, as "the mammoth project of the Mayor." But the scheme gradually expanded, until it embraced the opening of six new streets, and the erection of one of the finest and best appointed market-houses in the world. From beginning to end, Mr. Quincy was the soul of the enterprise; never discouraged, indefatigable, freely incurring personal responsibility when it was necessary to further the object. It was, therefore, with no ordinary satisfaction that he was able to

---

* Ibid., p. 102.

† Mr. Quincy had been led thoroughly to investigate the great questions connected with pauperism and crime, and indeed with the whole subject of social evils and abuses, before being called upon to carry his principles into effect. This appears from the "Address of the Board of Trustees of the Massachusetts General Hospital," written by him in 1814; his "Report to the Legislature on the Pauper Laws of Massachusetts," in 1821; his "Reports on the subject of Pauperism and a House of Industry in the Town of Boston," in the same year; and his "Remarks on some of the Provisions of the Laws of Massachusetts affecting Poverty, Vice, and Crime," in 1822. These, for the time, are full and instructive papers. In fact, when we remember how much Mr. Quincy wrote and did at that early day for the public health and comfort, and to prevent or repress mendicity and crime, especially among the young, and what opposition he met with and overcame, it seems to us that he is better entitled than any other person to be called the Father of Social Science in this country, — a science now in such vogue.

say, in his final Report on the subject, Nov. 13th, 1826, that
the noble improvement was completed; and this, too, without
any addition to the taxes or pecuniary burdens of the city,
present or to come.

If this were the place for a full account of Mr. Quincy's
mayoralty, it would be proper to speak of other things: especially of his efforts to extend the advantages of the public
schools; of his reconstruction of the fire department, then
for the first time made an independent and responsible body;
of his care to recover for the city an exclusive title to the
"Ropewalk Lands," west of Charles Street, now the Public
Garden; of the measures taken by him to defend the islands
in the harbor against the inroads of the sea; and of the first
movements towards supplying the city with water.*   It is
not meant that every thing done under Mr. Quincy's administration was done by him: on the contrary, he is eager, on
several occasions, to acknowledge important aid from other
members of the city government.   Still he was the chief
administrative and executive officer, and not a man to be so
in name without being so in reality.   Accordingly, it is impossible to review his course as Mayor without being convinced, that, owing partly to the time and circumstances in
which he entered on the office, and partly to his personal
qualities, the city, in its municipal capacity, is under more
and greater obligations to him, than to any other individual.

Nevertheless, he was aware from the outset, that a faith-
ful and uncompromising discharge of the duties of the chief
magistracy would give offence, not only to individuals, but
to whole classes.   In his first Inaugural Address, he intimated
that an amount of discontent would thus be gradually accumulated, which must sooner or later exclude him from
office.   And so it proved.   Twice he was re-elected, almost

---

* The first surveys and estimates for supplying Boston with water by aqueduct
were made by Professor Treadwell, at the request of Mr. Quincy, in 1825.

unanimously; but, after that, an organized and growing opposition began to manifest itself, which was at length successful.
When a candidate for the sixth time, in December, 1828, he
still had a decided plurality of the votes; but, after failing
on two trials to obtain the requisite majority, he definitively
withdrew. Mr. Quincy's own account of the whole affair, as
given in his "Address on Taking Final Leave of the Office of
Mayor," is characteristic.

"In all this there is nothing uncommon or unprecedented. The
public officer who, from a sense of public duty, dares to cross strong
interests in their way to gratification at the public expense, always has
had, and ever will have, meted to him the same measure. The beaten
course is, first to slander in order to intimidate; and, if that fail, then
to slander in order to sacrifice. He who loves his office better than
his duty, will yield and be flattered, — as long as he is a tool. He
who loves his duty better than his office will stand erect, — and take
his fate."

This is not the language of a demagogue, nor of a disappointed office-seeker; nor yet of an adroit politician: some,
indeed, may think that a more conciliating manner might
have saved his popularity, without involving any important
sacrifice of principle. However this may be, it is certain
that his most determined opponents never whispered against
him the charge of official corruption, or of selfish or by
ends; much less that of negligence or inaction. On the contrary, one of the principal complaints was, that he took too
much on himself; that he placed himself at the head of all
important Committees, and prepared all important Reports;
that there was no place which was not "vexed by his presence." To give a single example: it was his custom to mount
his horse at daybreak, and traverse the streets and lanes of
the city, that he might see every thing with his own eyes.
There were those, of course, to whom such incessant vigi-
lance and activity were unwelcome; and they revenged themselves by calling it "officiousness" and "intermeddling." So

far was this feeling carried, that, on one occasion, he was actually arraigned before the Police Court for fast riding, when
thus engaged in the public business, — to the danger, as it
was said, of other passengers. Two witnesses testified to the
fact. Mr. Quincy appeared, and pleaded " Not guilty," being
sure that no risk whatever had been incurred; at the same
time, he was willing that judgment should be entered against
him, and the fine and costs imposed, " to show that no individual could be placed above the law."

The only other popular topic insisted on against him was
the City Debt. Of course, it was impossible to carry through
the large public improvements instituted by him without large
public expenditure. Still he considered his defence complete,
inasmuch as he could say, that the taxes had not increased in
a ratio equal to the actual increase of property and population. Nay, more: he triumphantly asks, " Have I not a right
to assert, according to the usual and justifiable forms of expression under circumstances of this kind, that, so far as
respects the operations of the Administration now passing
away, they have left the city incumbered with NO DEBT ;
because they have left it possessed of a newly-acquired real
property, far greater, in marketable value, than the whole
debt it has incurred?" For these reasons, in concluding his
farewell Address, he did not hesitate to exclaim, in the noble
language used by the Hebrew magistrate on a similar occasion, " Behold! here I am : witness against me. Whom have
I defrauded? whom have I oppressed? at whose hands have
I received any bribe?"

Mr. Quincy was now fifty-seven years old. For most of
the time since arriving at manhood, he had held, as we have
seen, important civil trusts; but this did not hinder him from
taking an active part in the principal literary and scientific
associations of the day, and in all well-concerted measures for
the improvement of society, — a circumstance to be noticed
here, because it doubtless had quite as much to do in prepar-

ing the way, and suggesting his fitness, for his next appointment, as the public stations he had filled.

He was an early member of the American Academy of Arts and Sciences, and of the Massachusetts Historical Society. For many years he was a Trustee of Phillips Academy in Andover, and of the Theological Institution engrafted on it, and an Overseer of Harvard University. His duties at Washington, as a Representative in Congress, prevented him from being a member of the Anthology Club: but he was a zealous and liberal promoter of the Boston Athenæum, which grew out of that Club; and on leaving Congress, in 1813, he was made one of its Trustees. He was re-elected to this place, without intermission, for the next fifteen years; and for the last nine of them, and until his removal to Cambridge, he was President of the Institution. He also belonged to the first Board of Trustees of the Massachusetts General Hospital, and wrote the Address to the Public, in 1814, which resulted in raising the necessary funds for that noble charity. In 1824, Harvard College conferred on him the honorary degree of Doctor of Laws.

Nor should the military episode in Mr. Quincy's life be passed over in silence. It was in the disturbed times which preceded and attended our last war with England; when all thoughtful men felt the necessity there was to strengthen the hands of the government against invasion or insurrection from whatever quarter it might come. Under these circumstances, the Hussars, a troop of cavalry, splendidly mounted and equipped, was raised among the gentlemen of Boston and the vicinity in 1810, and Mr. Quincy was elected Captain. Afterwards he was promoted to the command of a squadron of horse, consisting of the Hussars and Dragoons, with the rank of Major. The Memoir, so often quoted, goes on to say, —

"His great personal advantages of face and figure, set off by his superb uniform, and by his fine charger ' Bayard,' white as snow, still dwell in the memory of the older inhabitants of Boston as the finest sight of man and horse they ever saw. At the peace, this corps was disbanded, its expensiveness being extreme; and he closed his military life. His horse 'Bayard,' oddly enough, was afterwards exported to Hayti, and became the favorite charger of the black king Christophe."

The ancestral estate in Quincy, bequeathed to him by his grandfather, came into his possession in 1798, and was ever afterwards, except while he was President of Harvard College, his summer residence. Here his attention was naturally turned to scientific and experimental farming, which he entered into, especially after resigning his seat in Congress, with his accustomed enthusiasm; his failures and successes, as is usual in such cases, being almost equally instructive to his neighbors and the public. He also became a leading member of the Massachusetts Agricultural Society, and contributed several valuable papers to the journal published under its auspices. Thus his year was about equally divided between his house in Boston and his house in Quincy, both of which were centres of a large and generous hospitality to his friends and to distinguished strangers. As his family were with him in his first winters at Washington, he had no occasion for his house in Pearl Street, before mentioned, and it was therefore leased, and never returned to. Afterwards, his town residence was successively in Oliver Street on Fort Hill, in Summer Street, and in Hamilton Place, — the last during his Mayoralty, and until his removal to Cambridge.

Dr. Kirkland had resigned the presidency of Harvard College in April, 1828. The place was still vacant at the end of the year, when, by the result of the election for Mayor in Boston, Mr. Quincy, as we have seen, was relieved from all public cares; and the attention of the Corporation was immediately turned on him as Dr. Kirkland's successor. He was chosen President of the University, January 15th, 1829. Up to this time, his mind had been mainly intent on political and civil affairs: for the sixteen years which followed, including all that remained of his public life, he threw himself, with characteristic singleness and earnestness of purpose, into his newly appointed work. It was a great change; and the feelings with which he contemplated it are best expressed in the following answer, under date of January 24th, to a very kind and cordial letter of welcome from the older Dr. Ware: —

"I need not say to you, Sir, how little the contemplated station has been to me an object of ambition, or even of desire. Not that it does not in itself include sufficient to render it a just object of the highest ambition and purest desire; but because, until it was proposed to me, it had never come within the scope of any thought or project of my life.

"When it was presented to my option, it was contemplated solely in the light of duty; and when my reflections resulted in a determination to accept, in case the appointing and sanctioning Boards should concur, I am not conscious that self-interest threw any weight into the preponderating scale. On the contrary, I feel that I am about to make great sacrifices of personal comfort, and to engage in new duties at a great disadvantage, both from my period of life and my previous habits, — that the result is dubious, as it respects not only my happiness, but my reputation.

"From all that I knew of the state of the interior of the Seminary, as well as from what I was apprized was seriously contemplated in this city, I could not but realize that the affairs of it were at a crisis, which made it the duty of every well-wisher to it to apply his strength in whatever way those intrusted with its superintendence deemed useful. Under the circumstances in which, by a singular course of Providence, I found myself placed, I could not refrain from believing that so extraordinary and unexpected a proposition, made at such a moment, indicated an imperious and not to be questioned duty.

"Throwing aside, therefore, personal considerations, and every other but this leading sense of obligation, I resolved, that, if called by the conjunct authorities of the University, I would undertake a task which I do not even yet know how it will be in my power to execute.

"I beg you, Sir, to be assured, and request you to assure the other gentlemen of the Faculty, that, if events should call me to that station, I shall enter upon it, pursuing no theories, subject to no schemes, with no projects; that I come free of pledge to change or to continue any thing that is done or in existence at the Seminary; and with a cordial desire to harmonize with, as I honor, every member of that Board. An absolute self-devotion to the interests of the Seminary is all that I promise."

The election of Mr. Quincy was confirmed by the Overseers, January 29th, and he was inaugurated with the customary formalities on Tuesday, the 2d of June.* Until the induction of President Kirkland, in 1810, all the inaugural exercises excepting the prayers, had been in Latin. With him began the practice of delivering the Inaugural Discourse in English; but neither his nor Mr. Quincy's was printed. The latter contained a forcible statement of the importance of adapting the methods and processes of education to the wants of the people and the spirit of the age; together with an earnest protest against an unreasonable urging of change, and the propensity in this country to multiply colleges, instead of building up and properly endowing a few.

At the inauguration, as well as in the letter just quoted and on other occasions, he speaks of his surprise on being called to preside over the University, and at the total change it would require in his habits of life, and this, too, at a somewhat advanced period of life. Nevertheless, it was a perfectly natural appointment. Mr. Quincy had always been a favorite and honored son of the University, and had stood up for her courageously, on more than one occasion, when her rights were threatened. He had also kept up his scholarly, and especially his classical, tastes and studies throughout all the vicissitudes of his public career, and, by his published

* The votes of the Overseers were forty for concurring, and twenty-six against it. The opposition was made up partly of those who objected to him on political or sectarian grounds, and partly of those who thought that the President of the College should be a clergyman, as had been the usage hitherto, with the single exception of Judge Leverett, and he was a Bachelor of Divinity, and had preached for a short period. The confirmation was strenuously resisted by writers in the "Boston Recorder" and the "Boston Statesman."

speeches, orations, addresses, and reports, and his contributions to the newspapers and magazines,* had won an acknowledged place among the literary men of the country. Nor should we forget in this connection the "Memoir" of his father, which he had given to the world in 1825, and of which Mr. Webster said, " It is one of the most interesting books I ever read, and brings me nearer than any other to the spirit which caused the American Revolution." Above all, he had a distinguished name and large connections and influence, and was known to be a man of experience and skill in affairs, of untiring assiduity, and of great vigor in government, — qualities in which the College was then supposed to be especially in want. A writer in the " Boston Statesman," though opposed to the appointment on sectarian grounds, felt obliged to say, " For Mr. Quincy I have a very high regard; and I think him possessed, in a high degree, of some of the qualifications for the chief executive office in the University. I utterly disclaim any design, in the remarks I am about to make, of calling in question his personal or literary qualifica-

---

* Newspaper "editorials," as they are now termed, were almost unknown in Mr. Quincy's early days, their place being supplied by articles, or series of articles, contributed anonymously, or under some popular pseudonym, by the leading and active minds of the day. Mr. Quincy did his full share of this work; but it is no longer easy to identify his contributions. The "Port Folio," in Philadelphia, was edited by his classmate, Joseph Dennie; and on this account, as well as from sympathy with its high political tone, he is supposed to have been a not unfrequent contributor to it. A long series of papers, headed "Climenole," and running through almost the whole of the fourth volume, for 1804, is ascribed to his pen. It is an ironical satire on the Democratic party, which probably had an interest and significance at the time, now lost. He also wrote occasionally for the "Monthly Anthology." He is the author of an extended and elaborate Review of Fisher Ames's Works, begun in the number for November, 1809, and continued through several successive numbers. Of course the article is highly laudatory: it could not be otherwise, in speaking of one of the greatest and best men this country has produced. But it is also discriminating, and shows a consciousness of the weak side of many of the Federal attacks on the dominant party. "He was," says the reviewer, "a partizan warrior, perpetually dashing into the very centre of the hostile camp, disturbing the sleep of the commander, and depriving his guards of repose; but the result of his efforts was rather brilliant than decisive. He brought away more marks of honor than trophies of victory; and obtained more evidences than rewards of prowess. His virtues and skill were the delight and admiration of his friends; but it does not appear that he made any durable impression on his enemies."

tions, or of making even an insinuation unfavorable to his character."

In one respect, however, he certainly was unprepared for his new duties, being without any experience whatever, either in the details of teaching or in the order and government of a large literary institution. As a practical man, he knew how serious this deficiency was; but he also knew in what way it could be supplied. For the first six months of his presidency, he gave himself entirely to the study of the processes of instruction and discipline, as they went on under his eyes; acting, meanwhile, under the constant advisement of Professor Ware, for whose judgment in these matters he always entertained the highest respect. It was not until after this, so far as the internal arrangements of the College were concerned, that he began to have an opinion of his own, and to cause his influence to be felt. It may also be mentioned, as illustrating his nice sense of justice, that, while Professor Ware was thus helping him to govern the College, he insisted on his receiving a portion of the President's salary.

With these qualifications, and in this spirit, he began his long administration, — only four of the twenty have been longer, — an administration which will ever hold an honorable place in the annals of the College, whether regard be had to its internal or external relations.

In what he did for its internal discipline, there was nothing which he looked back upon with more satisfaction than his success in introducing the practice of appealing to the laws of the land in cases of grave offence committed by members of the University. The measure had been resorted to before in rare and exceptional instances, but Mr. Quincy made it to be a part of the recognized policy of the College, and caused it to be inserted as such in the College Code. It was not so much for the purpose of bringing the students under new penalties, as of obtaining the means, through the grand jury,

of compelling testimony under oath, and so of bringing to light
the real culprits. Examinations before the Faculty were often
worse than useless. What was called "College morality"
justified all kinds of prevarication and subterfuge to screen
the guilty; or, if the witness shrank from such a course,
what was called "College honor," constrained him to refuse
to testify, thus taking the punishment on himself. In a long
address to the students, in October, 1829, announcing and recommending the new policy, he thus accounts for the origin
of these abuses:—

"The reason is, that youth are here denied the common principles
of examination and trial, by which alone truth can be maintained and
error detected. The Board charged with these investigations are en-
trusted with none of those powers by which alone society defends its
safety and property. Had the tribunals of justice no other means of
enforcing the discovery of truth than those possessed by the Faculty
of a college, society could not exist a day."

A few years afterwards, in the serious College disturbances of 1834, the courts of law were again resorted to, and
indictments were found against three students. The proceed-
ing occasioned some uneasiness, as well within as without
academic circles, and was finally brought up for consideration
before the Overseers; which led Mr. Quincy to undertake before that Board a still more elaborate defence of the policy
in question. In the course of the argument he observes,—

"Farther reflection, however, led to the conclusion that the so-called
'College morality' itself, complained of above, was not so much the
effect of any peculiar perversity in the youthful mind, arising from
influences existing within the sphere of a college, as the natural and
even necessary consequence of a pretended immunity from the laws of
the State. When once the certainty of being examined under oath
and confronted with each other, as in courts of justice, is established,
the power of obtaining impunity by falsehood is taken away, and with
this the temptation to commit it. Of all principles of moral corruption, in youth or manhood, that is the surest and most effectual which
places the individual above or beyond the sanctions of the law." . . .

"The notion that this exemption from the laws of the land is a privilege to students, is of all opinions the most false and fallacious. A privilege! To whom? Not to the orderly and well-disposed. To these it is an oppressive and insupportable evil. By the effect of such exemption they are deprived of the character of compelled witnesses, and obliged to take that of voluntary informers, if they speak the truth."

The whole subject was then referred by the Overseers to a Committee, John Quincy Adams being the chairman, who, in an able and extended report, approved of every thing which the President and Faculty had done; and the resolutions embodying the sense of the report were "unanimously" adopted by the Board.* The good effects of the new determination were not, perhaps, so immediate or so considerable as expected: up to this hour, indeed, it has been but imperfectly carried out; but there can be no doubt that it was the beginning of a more efficient administration of college discipline. It is probably one of the causes which, for a quarter of a century, have prevented the recurrence of an open and general "rebellion" against the College authorities, — formerly so frequent, almost periodic. It is also thought to have done much to save the College from those violent collisions between officers and students, sometimes ending in homicide, by which similar institutions in this country have been troubled. In every instance of mere college mischief,

---

* Alluding in the Report to certain strictures which the Senior Class had seen fit, in their published account of the disturbances, to pass on the Head of the College, Mr. Adams says, "For nearly five and forty years, since President Quincy took, as a member of the then Senior Class of Harvard University, at the close of his career as a student, the highest honors of the Seminary, his life, his deportment, his manners, may emphatically be said to have been exhibited in the presence of all his brethren. The life of no man of his cotemporaries has been more constantly under the eye of the public. It is not for this Committee to pronounce his panegyric: to many members of this Board he was long familiarly and intimately known, before any one member of the present Senior Class of Harvard University was born. He was known to their fathers, — known to many of their grandsires, in multiplied relations of life, public and private. It was reserved for the circular of the Senior Class of Harvard University to convey, in doubting and dubious terms, an imputation upon his sincerity and integrity."

7

the prosecution has led to confession; whereupon the prosecution has been withdrawn, the College falling back on college punishments as soon as the real culprits were known.

There was another subject intimately connected with the peace of the College and its proper relations to the community, by which Mr. Quincy's mind was much exercised. It will be remembered that the people were beginning, at this time, to be divided and intensely exasperated on a multitude of new questions and new projects. In the ordinary relations of life, he was not a man, as we have seen, to counsel or practise timid reserves or a non-committal policy. But he felt that a retreat for study should be kept as far removed as possible from the noisy and distracting strifes of the hour. Moreover, he was eminently a just man. He knew that he had no right to use the influence, or complicate the interests and prospects of a great public institution placed under his care, as he might his own. He knew that Harvard College belonged to no party, or sect, or clique; and he therefore strove, both by example and authority, to keep it free from all such entanglements on the one side or the other.

Thus, in 1838, having been informed that a discussion was announced for the evening, in some society belonging to the Divinity School, "on the subject of 'Abolition,' as it is called," and that very general invitations had been given to the undergraduates, and to the members of the respective schools, to attend on the occasion, he hastened to apprise the Theological Faculty of the fact, and to express his regret and concern on account of it. In the course of this communication he observes: " Whatever may be your or my private opinion on the main question, I think there can be but one in the minds of prudent men, that, in the state of excessive excitability of the public mind on this topic abroad, it is desirable not to introduce it obtrusively into a seminary of learning, composed of young men from every quarter of the country; among whom are many whose prejudices, passions, and inter-

ests are deeply implicated and affected by these discussions,
and who feel very naturally and strongly on the subject."
Again, in 1840, he writes to a tutor, reminding him of the
circumstances which attended his appointment: "I then distinctly stated to you, that there was no sense of official duty
more imperative in my mind than that of keeping Harvard
College out of *every party vortex*, and that I held it an incum-
bent duty of every officer of the Institution to abstain from
any act tending to bring within its walls discussions upon
questions on which the passions and interests of the community are divided, and warmly engaged, without doors."

For several years, many of the friends of the College had
been urging important reforms in its course and methods of
instruction, rendered necessary, as it was said, by the wants
of the community and the advanced state of science. Little, however, had as yet been done towards maturing these
schemes, and carrying them into effect; and one of the hopes
entertained on the appointment of Mr. Quincy was, that they
would soon begin to feel the effects of that indomitable spirit
of activity and progress which he had just been evincing as
Mayor. And this hope was not disappointed. In June, 1830,
he submitted to the Board of Overseers "A General Plan of
Studies," designed "chiefly to effect a more thorough education in the Greek and Latin languages, the Mathematics,
and Rhetoric." According to the new program, the hours
given to the first three studies above mentioned are nearly
doubled, without lessening the amount of instruction in the
other departments. Here, certainly, was early evidence of
activity and progress; but not, it must be confessed, in the
popular direction. Most of the reformers believed that abundant time was given already to mathematical and classical
studies: what they wanted was, that more room should be
made, at least for such as desired it, for the moral and physical sciences and the modern languages. They demanded, in
short, that a much larger privilege of selection among dif-

ferent studies should be allowed; that classes should be
divided into sections, according to talent and proficiency;
that examinations should be rendered more thorough and
effective; that rank should be determined by a carefully and
elaborately prepared scale of merit; and that the College
should be open to students wishing to avail themselves of
its means of instruction in particular departments, without
being candidates for a degree.*

Mr. Quincy is understood to have had his doubts, from
the beginning, as to the wisdom or practicability of some
of these propositions. Nevertheless, as they had been repeatedly recommended and insisted on, and sometimes by
the authorities of the College, he was sincerely desirous,
acting in concert with the Faculty, to put them to the test
of experience. And it was remarkable in Mr. Quincy, that,
whenever he felt called upon to execute a plan, he threw
his whole soul into it, forgetting all objections and misgivings
he may himself have once entertained, and acting as if the
entire scheme, from its inception, was his own. This appears
in the course he took in 1832, respecting what was then
called, "The Minimum Scheme." It consisted in establishing a *minimum* in every important branch, which was required of all as the condition of a degree. But "any number
of students in any class, not less than six, wishing to attain
this minimum in an early part of the College course, might
form a section for that purpose." Having effected this object,
they were free to elect what studies they would afterwards

---

* See on this subject a Report of a Committee of the Overseers in 1824, of which
Judge Story and Mr. John Pickering were active members; "Remarks on a Report of
a Committee of the Overseers of Harvard College, proposing certain Changes in the Instruction and Discipline of the College. By One, lately a Member of the Immediate
Government" [Professor Norton], 1824; "Remarks on Changes lately proposed or
adopted in Harvard University. By George Ticknor, Smith Professor, &c.," 1825;
"Speech of John Pickering, Esq., before the Board of Overseers," published in the
"American Statesman," for Feb. 1, 1825; and an article on "Reform of Harvard College," in the "United-States Literary Gazette," begun June 15, and continued through
successive issues to Dec. 1, 1825, by Dr. Gamaliel Bradford.

pursue, and " be formed into sections in reference to those studies, *without regard to classes*." Again, in the following year, he was equally in earnest for another plan, which consisted in confining the required study of Greek, Latin, and Mathematics to the Freshman and Sophomore Classes, so that students who were unprepared in those studies might enter the Junior Class, and take a two-years' college course in Intellectual, Moral, and Political Philosophy, in the Physical Sciences, and in the Modern Languages. The latter would not be entitled to a degree; but, in lieu thereof, they were to receive a diploma specifying what they had done.

Both of these projects fell through, because they were found to require a larger staff of instruction than the College had at its disposal. But in other respects he was more successful; especially in the measures agreed upon to secure a perfectly reliable scale of merit, an improved method of public examinations, and a large extension of the elective system. For a time, indeed, the elective system was carried so far as to allow any student to discontinue the study of Greek, Latin, and Mathematics, one or all, *at the end of the Freshman year*, choosing a substitute out of several studies proposed, among which were the Modern Languages. Many were alarmed at this bold innovation, thinking it little better than an abandonment of the classics altogether; so much so, that Mr. Quincy felt called upon to come forward in its defence, in " Remarks on the Nature and Probable Effects of introducing the Voluntary System," addressed to the Board of Overseers, in 1841. He argues thus: —

" Now, what possible objection can there be to permitting parents or guardians, who know the character, aptitudes, and destination of their sons or wards, to decide the question for them ? Is it possible, in the nature of things, that what is best in every individual case can be better decided by the principles of a general system than by the intelligence of the natural guardians of a young man, acting upon a knowledge of his peculiar powers, temperament, and objects in life?

If a parent chooses that his son shall not spend more than one college
year in imbuing his mind with a knowledge of Greek and Latin, what
concern has the College or the friends of classical literature in the
matter, provided he do not obstruct others in attaining it? How
much less concern, then, have they, — rather, how much reason to encourage and rejoice in this voluntary secession from these studies, when
the direct effect must be to aid, and take obstructions from the path of,
those who engage ardently in the pursuit of these languages! . . .

"A college which should send forth only two-thirds, or even one-
half, of its graduates, thoroughly educated by a known and seen standard, by which they were faithfully tried and rejected if found wanting,
and if approved receive the appropriate honor, will do more *for the
cause of classical learning*, than twenty colleges who send forth all
their members tried by no standard, without any evidence of attain-
ment, except having passed through a prescribed process, and where
what they have done is matter of faith and not of sight."

If it should still be objected that he did not do as much as
was expected for academic reform, the answer is found in the
fact that he did more than the College has been able to retain. At the present moment, though a re-action is understood to be now going on in favor of the elective or proper
University system, that principle is not carried out and applied to any thing like the same extent as under President
Quincy's administration. Moreover, we must not shut our
eyes to another fact, — namely, that there was, and is, a serious difficulty in the way, though one, we are glad to say, that
is continually lessening.* A large proportion of our Fresh-

* In the four consecutive years, beginning with 1806, the average age of students
entering Harvard College, was sixteen years and four months; in the four consecutive
years beginning with 1820, it was sixteen years and eleven months; in the four consecutive years beginning with 1860, it was seventeen years and eight months. But there
is another view to be taken of the comparative age of the students, which makes the
change more noteworthy. In the first two of the above-mentioned groups of classes,
many entered under fifteen, and nearly half under sixteen; while in the last, out of four
hundred and seventy-seven admitted, there was but one under fifteen, and only eighteen
under sixteen. This change has been brought about, for the most part, by the higher
character and greater strictness of the examination for admission; but, if more is now
exacted, it is almost exclusively in one branch, the ancient languages, and is not understood to involve any essential change of general policy. A vast amount of rudimental

man and Sophomore Classes, whether regard be had to their age or studies, ought rather to be at some public school or gymnasium. The instruction required, or most of it at least, might be given there to better advantage, at less expense, and with far less moral exposure. As things now are, it may certainly be said, with no little show of reason, of these classes at least, that they have not as yet completed the general and preliminary studies which are necessary to a liberal education; and therefore that, for them, the time has not come to talk about dropping one study, and taking up another. And besides, even if they were to do so, who supposes that the mere right of selection among a crowd of *elementary* studies will make a university? Undoubtedly these elementary studies must first be attended to and mastered; but a university is not the place for it. Whenever Harvard College is ready to take the stand of leaving all rudimentary and drill teaching to the preparatory seminaries, and open its doors wide to persons of maturity, and to them alone, — that is to say, to persons who must be presumed to know what high special teaching they are fitted for and require, — the Voluntary or Elective System, without restriction or limita-

---

instruction is still expected and provided for in the College: it is, however, an important gain, that more than a year has been added to the average age of the students.

Some are disposed to counsel contentment with things as they are, on the ground, that, as our colleges have grown up amidst our wants, they must be suited to them. But this is a fallacy. Though our colleges have grown up amidst our wants, they have never been what the country really required, but only what it was in a condition to do for the time being, — a compromise between our wants and our means. Again, there are those who are willing that the College should sink into a mere preparatory department for the Professional and Scientific Schools, the latter to be regarded as the University proper. But the sons of Harvard will be slow to acquiesce in this view. It is hardly necessary to add, that the advocates of change have no wish to slight or crowd out the classics and the pure mathematics: on the contrary, they would provide the means of a much higher instruction in both, as well as in every other branch of liberal culture, for such as wish it, and will give the time to it. As for what is said about the disciplinary effect of different studies, it applies almost exclusively to boys. After the mind has attained a certain degree of maturity and independence, we suspect that the amount of intellectual discipline any study affords will depend in no small measure on the interest taken in it, or the preference from some cause felt for it; in short, on the student's " working with a will."

tion, will follow as a matter of course, and the College will become a proper university; — then, and except in a very imperfect degree, not until then.

We have dwelt on Mr. Quincy's efforts to improve the discipline and instruction of the College proper, because this was a care that was always on his mind; but it did not tempt him to overlook or neglect any other branch or interest of the University. Witness the new impulse which was almost immediately given to the Law School. Provision had been made, it is true, several years before, for giving legal instruction in the University; and this had been done with ability and success, but on a comparatively limited scale. The Law School, as at present constituted, may be said to date from the inauguration of Judge Story and Mr. Ashmun as professors, which took place Aug. 25, 1829, — a few months after President Quincy entered upon office. He had much to do with the change; and it was also owing, in no small measure, to his activity and perseverance, that funds were found for the erection of Dane Hall, in 1832. Writing, about this time, to the Hon. Nathan Dane, of Beverly, who had founded a new professorship, and after whom the new Hall was named, he says, "The School is flourishing beyond all expectation. It already consists of thirty-five members. Five or six more are known to contemplate joining it, and others are anticipated. We think ourselves justified in calculating with certainty on forty members, and I have reason to think it will exceed that number." Before Mr. Quincy resigned his office, the number had grown to be one hundred and sixty-three, collected from almost every State in the Union.

His attention was soon drawn to another important object. The College Library, which had become considerable, and the loss of which would have been in some respects irretrievable, was still in the upper story of Harvard Hall, where it was neither conveniently nor safely provided for. He saw that a new building had become necessary; and his first step

was to importune the Legislature for aid in erecting it; —
urging, among other things, that the first library of the College had been burnt, in 1764, together with the Hall in which
it was deposited, while the latter was in temporary occupation by the General Court; and further, that the benefits of
the Library, when increased as it was likely to be, would not
accrue to the College alone, but to all scholars, and the public
generally. Meeting, however, with no response from that
quarter, he reluctantly consented, and induced a majority of
the Corporation to consent, that a great part of Mr. Gore's
large bequest, which was shackled by no conditions, should
be devoted to this purpose. To him, therefore, under these
circumstances, the College is indebted for Gore Hall, which
was built in the years 1839–42.

Another subject on which Mr. Quincy's thoughts were much
occupied during the last years of his presidency, and indeed
to the end of his life, was the Astronomical Observatory. A
movement had been made by the Corporation as early as
1815, probably the earliest in the country, for the establishment of such an institution; and another, in 1822; but neither
was followed up by the energy necessary to success. Mr.
Quincy, in a letter to John Quincy Adams, who had been
among the most active in recommending the former attempts,
gives the following account of the first steps taken by
himself:—

"Early in the year 1839, the President of the University being
informed that Mr. William Cranch Bond was engaged, under con-
tract with the government of the United States, in a series of astronomical, meteorological, and magnetic observations at Dorchester,
with reference to the Exploring Expedition of the United States then
in the Southern Ocean, it occurred to him, that if Mr. Bond could be
induced to transfer his residence and apparatus to Cambridge, and
pursue his observations there under the auspices of the University, it
would have an important influence in clearing the way for an establishment of an efficient Observatory in connection with that seminary,

8

·by the increase of the apparatus at its command, by the interest
which the observations making by Mr. Bond were calculated to excite; and, by drawing the attention of the citizens of Boston and its
vicinity to the great inadequacy of the means possessed by the University for efficient astronomical observations, create a desire and a
disposition to supply them."

Every thing succeeded according to his wishes and expectations. Mr. Bond removed to Cambridge, where a temporary
observatory had been fitted up for him in connection with the
Dana House, situated within the college grounds. The necessary funds were immediately raised for purchasing additional
instruments; and a much larger sum soon afterwards, for
erecting and equipping the present noble Observatory, which,
under the direction of the two Bonds, father and son, has
already reflected so much credit on the College and on American science. Ground was broken for laying the foundation of
the central pier, Aug. 15, 1843. To defray the current ex-
penses of the establishment, the College received, in 1848,
a bequest of a hundred thousand dollars from Mr. Edward
Bromfield Phillips, a kinsman and former ward of Mr. Quincy; and ten thousand dollars were also given by himself to
the same object.*

Time would fail, were we to undertake a full enumeration
of the benefits accruing to Harvard College under President
Quincy's administration. He found the whole number of
students on his accession to office to be, including all departments of the University, four hundred and one; when he left,
it was six hundred and twenty-one. He found a corps of

---

* Mr. Quincy's donation was in fulfilment of his father's bequest of £2,000 ster-
ling to the College, in case his son should die a minor. He used to say that the
College should not be a loser for his unreasonableness in outliving the prescribed term.
The donation makes part of the Publishing Fund of the Observatory; and he directed
that the following insertion should be made in the titlepage of every volume, the
expense of which is defrayed from this source: "Printed from Funds resulting from
the Will of Josiah Quincy, Jun., who died in April, 1775, leaving a Name inseparably
connected with the History of the American Revolution." The whole transaction was
very characteristic of the donor.

twenty-one professors and teachers; he left a corps of twenty-
nine. He found the College yard a narrow and irregular strip
of land, less than two-thirds of what it is at present: he left
it not only greatly enlarged, but bounded on all sides by
public streets. He found the financial concerns of the College
in considerable embarrassment: he left them in perfect order.
He found the productive funds of the University amount-
ing to $450,903.90: he left them amounting to $706,615.24.
Here too, without question, much was due to the ability
and faithfulness of his colleagues in the government; still, as
was said before, Mr. Quincy was not a man to be nominally
the efficient and controlling head of an institution without
being really so.

In the discharge of the current duties of his office as
President of the University, he was as prompt, as unwearied,
and as punctilious, as he had been in every previous public
trust. An opinion had long prevailed, which was expressed
and dwelt upon in the Report to the Overseers in 1824, that
the President should be relieved " from the performance of
merely ministerial duties," such as granting leave of absence,
and attending to ordinary matters of discipline. But Mr.
Quincy was the last man in the world to ask for or accept
an exemption from work or care or responsibility, under
whatever shape it might come. Even the details, the routine
of the office, irksome as they have been thought, had a sort of
fascination for his intensely active nature; and he would listen
to no suggestions of curtailment or assistance. He was always in his place. For sixteen years he was never absent
from the College chapel at morning prayers but once, and
then on account of necessary absence from town on College
business. Probably it was this entering into, and identifying
himself with, every measure and movement of the University
that rendered him so sensitive to attacks upon it. If more of
these attacks had been left unnoticed, it might, perhaps, have
been as well; especially when, as was sometimes the case,

they originated in political or religious jealousies, which it
was impossible either to silence or allay. All that many
of the assailants hoped for was to raise a question and call
forth an answer, knowing how injurious it is to an individual
or an institution to be frequently coming before the public as
defendant, no matter how able and successful each particular
defence may be.

But there was one instance in which his opposition to en-
croachments on the settled policy of the College deserves particular mention, as it gave him an opportunity to express his
profound sense of the obligations the College has been under
to the Congregational clergy from its earliest days, and also to
show that he was not one of those who are carried away
by every new cry of "liberality." Until 1834, clergymen,
to be eligible to the Board of Overseers, must be Congregationalists; but an Act was passed by the Legislature of that
year, opening the Board to clergymen of all denominations, —
the Act to take effect whenever accepted by both branches
of the College government. That little or no general interest was taken in the proposition is evident from the fact,
that it was allowed to slumber in the statute-book for nearly
nine years, without inquiry or complaint from any quarter.
At length a vote of the Overseers called the attention of the
President and Fellows to the existence of this law, with a
request that they would take the initiative on the question
of its acceptance. Under these circumstances, Mr. Quincy
brought up the subject for consideration, declaring, at the
same time, his own opinion in a written and elaborate argument against the measure; in which, as usual, he is not a
whit the less decided and confident, though perfectly aware
the effort would be of no avail, and that he was likely to
stand, as in fact he did, almost alone. As this document has
never been printed, an extract or two, illustrative of his
views of the external relations of the University, will not
be improper.

"The whole history of Massachusetts," as he tells us, "bears witness to the instrumentality of the Congregational clergy in founding and upholding Harvard College. With them originated the first conception of the design. By their influence, which was scarcely less than conclusive with the first settlers of the Colony, its statesmen were induced to extend to it the degree of favor which they did. For one hundred and fifty years they were intrusted with its chief care and management. When it became necessary, in the Convention of 1780, to declare who should be the successors of the Board of Overseers established under the ancient charters of the College, the framers of the Constitution ordained, in conformity with those charters, that the ministers of the Congregational churches therein specified should still constitute the clerical part of that Board. Nor did the act of 1810 make any alteration in this respect, but continued the Congregational order in its long-established clerical relations and rights, — enlarging rather than restricting them. . . .

"Thus the right in question is granted to the Congregational order by all the charters of the institution. It is a right which the present members of that order and their predecessors have attained, not through any party spirit or favoritism, but from the fact that they were originally the efficient founders of the College, and have, in all times, by their zeal, labors, and influence, been greatly instrumental in promoting its growth and prosperity. Now, where do the Overseers and the Corporation obtain the power to deprive the great Congregational Order of Massachusetts of this right, so honorably won and maintained? . . .

"But, it has been said, this change will not materially affect the influence of the Congregational clergy; that it will still depend upon the votes of the Board of Overseers, whether any other and what denominations shall be admitted, and that they will of course restrict the selection to such as will harmonize with them. All this is very smooth and lubricating. But powers which are sought are generally intended to be used. Accretion and extension are inherent in the very nature of power. If 'liberality' requires that all denominations should be made eligible to the Board of Overseers, it also requires, just as much, that every denomination should be represented in it. And it cannot be doubted, that, on every occurrence of a clerical vacancy in the Board, the friends of every sect will put in its claim; and, if denied, there will result a great clamor about 'illiberality.' So that they who are for accepting this act will find to their cost, that, instead of attaining their end, they have perpetuated the very evil they would avoid upon themselves, and entailed it on their successors."

Experience did not verify these apprehensions: the College continued to flourish under the new order of things. Still, in these days of hankering after change and a more æsthetic worship, it is a satisfaction to know that there was one man who never forgot that his ancestors were Congregationalists, and who had the courage, in the face of all the popular tendencies, to stand up for what he believed to be the rights of the Congregational clergy, — a body of men, to whom, with all their faults, New England is mainly indebted for what is most distinctive in its history, institutions, and character.

Amidst his many official cares, little and great, President Quincy found time for no inconsiderable amount of literary work. In 1830 he delivered an "Address to the Citizens of Boston on the Close of the Second Century from the First Settlement of the City." It is one of the most carefully prepared, and most discriminating and valuable, of all his public addresses. He was also called, Sept. 8, 1836, at the close of the second century after the foundation of the College, to deliver a discourse in commemoration of that event. The latter, though eloquent and elaborate in itself, was chiefly remarkable for having suggested and prepared the way for his extended History of the institution. After having glanced at the four great periods, under which the events affecting the fortunes of the College may be conveniently arranged and considered, he thus proceeds:—

"From this view it is apparent, that the occasion requires, not an oration, but a treatise; not an address, but a HISTORY.

"Like the historian, then, of ancient times, when, on Grecian soil and like solemn occasion, were assembled, as now and here, the wise, the learned, the pious, and the great, let us also strive to beguile the passing hour with an appropriate story of former years; and like him,

too, leave it half told, when hearers give signs of weariness, or when
the herald shall proclaim that the time has come for the feast and the
games."

His "History of Harvard University" did not appear until 1840. It was a labor of love. The records and archives
of the College were all open to him; and no expense was
spared in order to make this work the most acceptable and
enduring monument of his devotion to his Alma Mater. It
fills two large octavo volumes, and, in point of mechanical
execution, is still universally regarded as one of the most
beautiful and perfect productions of the American press.
The first impression of seven hundred and fifty copies, including the whole charge for the stereotype plates, cost
above six thousand dollars. Having no view to pecuniary
emolument, Mr. Quincy, at the outset, made over his property in the work to the College, guaranteeing it in any event
against loss, and providing that the profits, if any, should
accrue to the funds for assisting indigent students. After
the first and principal sales had been effected, the balance
against the work, from various unforeseen causes, amounted
to between three and four thousand dollars, which was
promptly paid by the author, leaving the College in possession of the remaining copies and the stereotype plates, free
of all expense.

The History was cordially welcomed by the friends of the
College, and especially by those most conversant with its
interests and traditions. The Hon. Daniel Appleton White,
to make room for one among many, writes thus: —

"By combining with your narrative of University concerns a variety
of important public topics, and arranging them judiciously, with lively
and graphic sketches of character, you have made your work exceed-
ingly attractive to all readers of American history and literature. . . .
You have presented a striking and most satisfactory view of the
ecclesiastical history of Massachusetts, — the most so. indeed, that I
recollect to have met with. Some persons may remain who will be

at first shocked at the picture drawn of the two Mathers and of Han-
cock, if not of a few others; but in this the author of the History
cannot be blamed, as it must be perceived the portraits are of their
own drawing. Nothing can be more manifest to the reader of this
History than the author's determined spirit of candor, justice, and fidel-
ity, as well as of independence." *

Now that first impressions have given place to calm and
mature judgment, we are in a condition to speak with more
confidence and discrimination of the merits of this work. In
the first place, every student of history will know how to
appreciate the Appendixes to the two volumes, embracing, as
they do, a large collection of interesting and important docu-
ments, which are thus saved, and in some cases, it might
almost be said, redeemed from destruction. Turning, next,
to the History itself, all again must agree in according to it
the qualities of a permanent and standard work. The author,
it is true, wrote too eagerly and too rapidly for one who
would become a model of exactness and finish: his mind was
taken up by other things; nevertheless, his diction is always
clear, strong, and idiomatic, rising at times into a genuine,
because spontaneous, eloquence; and distinguished throughout by a certain air of independence and nobility, which

* We cannot refrain from subjoining the testimony of a foreigner, Mr. James
Grahame, the author of "The History of the United States." In a letter to Mr. Quincy,
from Nantes, July, 1841, he says: "As you advance, you wound some of my preju-
dices. The Mathers are very dear to me; and you attack them with a severity the
more painful to me that I am unable to demur to its justice. I would fain think that
you do not make sufficient allowance for the spirit of the times. My heart and judgment are with them in point of doctrine. From their view of discipline my judgment
utterly revolts." Again, writing to Mr. Quincy's daughter in the following October,
he observes: "Since my return from my late travels, I have thoroughly read your
father's 'History of Harvard University,' often with pleasure, sometimes with pain, —
always with final, deep, austere satisfaction and approbation. ... No other country
than your own ever produced a seat of learning so honorable to its founders and early
supporters as Harvard University; and never did a noble institution obtain a worthier
historian. ... His account of the transition of the social system of Massachusetts from
an entire and punctilious intertexture of Church and State to the restriction of municipal government to civil offices and occupations, is very curious and interesting, and
admirably well fills up an important void in New-England history."

marked his style as well as his thoughts, and indeed his whole character. Then, too, it is quite plain that the records and archives of the University have been thoroughly explored for information respecting its internal history; by which is meant the changes in its internal constitution, its methods of instruction and discipline, and its standard of scholarship at different periods. It is doubtless to be regretted that the result is often so meagre and unsatisfactory; still we have all, or nearly all, the light on these subjects to be gathered from the books and papers of the College. More might perhaps have been done to fill out the picture from other sources; and there are those, probably, who would have liked the history better if it had been written on this principle, and in the spirit of an academic and literary antiquary. But such a work was not, of course, to be expected from Mr. Quincy. All his tastes and habits of thought, as a public man, had led him to be chiefly interested in the external history of the College; that is to say, in the history of its governors rather than of its teachers and teaching, and in its relations to public affairs, and to the rivalships and struggles of the leading men in Church and State.

By thus following his natural bent, he has doubtless given to the work a peculiar interest and importance; but with the inconvenience, that he often found himself on debatable ground, where, take whatever position he might, he was sure to be met by the stock objections on the other side.* Something must also be pardoned to an ardent mind, which is apt

---

* Two articles containing strictures on the work appeared in the sixth and seventh volumes of the "American Biblical Repository," — namely, a "Review of Quincy's History of Harvard University. By One of the Professors of Yale College" (Professor Kingsley); and an "Examination of Certain Points in New-England History, as exhibited by President Quincy in his History of Harvard University, and by other Unitarian Writers. By Enoch Pond, D.D." It was favorably noticed by the Rev. Dr. Parkman, in the "Christian Examiner" for March, 1841, and also, though with some discriminations, by Dr. Palfrey, in the "North American Review" for April in the same year.

to see things through an intensifying medium.. Not that he confounded white with black, or black with white; but his white was sometimes a little whiter, and his black a little blacker, than the reality. Add to this, that, misled by approved authorities, he has fallen into some errors of fact; for instance, as to the influence of Sewell and Addington in framing the Charter of Yale College, and perhaps in some of his statements respecting the Mathers. But none of these things affect, in any manner or degree, his great argument; which shows, that, for the last century and a half, Harvard College has been under the constant patronage and control of what may be called the liberal party of Massachusetts, using the term "liberal" to denote, not the opinions held, but the spirit in which they were held. Down to a comparatively recent date, the governors and teachers of the College were Orthodox Congregationalists. If it has since passed, to a certain extent, under other influences, we have no right to say that it has passed into other hands. The change in the College was preceded or attended by a like change in the surrounding community. The very same class of men who have had ascendency in the College for many generations, and who have made it what it is, have ascendency still; the only difference being, that the minds of this class have gradually become more and more liberal in spirit, and many of them also in doctrine.

At one time Mr. Quincy had it in view to reply to the exceptions taken to his History. But he soon perceived that these exceptions related, for the most part, to inferences respecting character and motives, the justice or injustice of which his readers were already in a condition to determine for themselves. Or if, in a few cases, they extended to facts, it was, as a general rule, simply because these facts were regarded from a different point of view and with different prepossessions. Under these circumstances, the continuance of the discussion was not likely to be of any avail; and, besides, it would require that almost every question involved in the study of the early history of New England should be re-opened, — a useless and thankless task, to which he did not feel himself to be called. He begins a manuscript containing some brief and unfinished notices of his reviewers with these solemn asseverations: —

"If ever a work was written with an entire independence of any design to shape the course of the narrative to favor or disparage any religious sect or opinion, it was that work. For, so far as any human being is conscious, or has a right to speak, concerning his own state of mind or motive, I was utterly indifferent to the whole controversy. . . . I have no intention to enter into a controversy, in the results of which I have no interest, and concerning which, owing to the length and number of the discussions on the subject, almost any thing may be asserted, and almost any thing denied. All differences about the character and conduct of individuals are fair subjects of criticism and contradiction. On re-examining them, so far as my History is concerned, I see nothing to retract."

Again, in answering a letter from a friend some years afterwards, he writes as follows: —

"You have several times intimated to me a wish, that, previously to publishing a second edition of my ' History of Harvard College,' I would review and consider the objections which have been made to some of my conclusions and inferences concerning the history of the period to which it relates, affecting sometimes the character of men and sometimes of parties, varying from, if not offending, the preju-dices or the sentiments of one or both the sectarian divisions which exist in our Commonwealth. Almost all these objections, as far as in the course of their publication they have come to my knowledge, I have already considered, and they are generally of a nature which I cannot hope to overcome ; being, for the most part, the result of theological opinions, or connected with sectarian interests, which nothing can satisfy but victory."

Mr. Quincy resigned the presidency of the College, Aug. 27, 1845, at the age of seventy-three, — his bodily faculties but little affected by his years, and his mind not at all. He

now returned to his former mode of life, passing his winters
in Boston, and his summers on his estate in Quincy; but with
this difference, that, being relieved from all public cares, he
could bestow his time as he pleased. Not a day, however,
was lost. As soon as he found himself on his farm again, his
old fondness for agricultural pursuits came back in all its
freshness; and the more so, as he believed these pursuits to
afford the fittest occupation for an old man, — interesting
without being exciting, and deriving their interest from
causes which have nothing to do with the strifes and ambi-
tions of the world. What makes it more remarkable is, that
he was able, at his advanced age, not only to take the entire
management of the farm into his own hands, but to retain it
for more than ten years; during which he was as intent as
ever on new improvements, and as eager as ever to recommend them in conversation and by his pen. Nor was this all.
It was at this period, and under these circumstances, that he
added largely to his fortune by a bold and successful specu-
lation, from which younger men shrunk, and the details of
which are equally creditable to his foresight and to his public
spirit. In the words of his son, —

"When Mayor, he had built a wharf, called the City Wharf, which
belonged to the City, and which from its position he thought should
always be held by it; and this opinion he had left on record at the
time. When he was more than eighty, the City Government proposed
selling this property. Mr. Quincy remonstrated against it in the
papers and by memorial, setting forth the reasons why it was important that the control of that particular piece of property should be
retained by the City. The authorities, however, proceeded with their
scheme; and at the sale he appeared, and bid it off. Having thus the
control of it, he wrote to the Mayor, offering to re-convey it to the City
if it would bind itself not to sell it again for twenty years. The
City refused, and he retained the property."

Still, it was among his books, pen in hand, that most of his
hours were passed. Long after he had attained to an age in

which most persons find a reason or an excuse for leaving off
work altogether, he was wont to regard it as a broken day if
he were not busily engaged in his library from nine o'clock
in the morning to nine in the evening. Nor were his studies
without object, or without fruit. In 1847, when he was
seventy-five, appeared his "Life and Journals of Major
Samuel Shaw." This was followed, four years afterwards,
by his "History of the Boston Athenæum, with Biographical
Notices of its Deceased Founders." In 1852, at the close
of his eightieth year, he published his "Municipal History
of the Town and City of Boston." Finally, in 1858, in his
eighty-seventh year, appeared his "Memoir of the Life of
John Quincy Adams." Each of these works fills an octavo
volume, and must have required a large amount of literary
labor; yet they betray, to the last, but little if any decay of
intellectual vigor. The last work especially, if we consider
the difficulty and delicacy of the task, and the success with
which it is executed, in connection with the extreme age of
the author, is almost without a parallel. To these must also
be added a "Memoir of James Grahame," the historian, and a
"Memoir of John Bromfield," published during the same
period; together with several political and controversial
pamphlets, called forth by the exigency of the times, — all
of which are full of life, and often as effective and trenchant
as the productions of his best days.*

There was a time, as before intimated, when Mr. Quincy

* Among these are found the following : "Considerations submitted to the Citizens
of Boston and Charlestown on the proposed Annexation of these two Cities," 1854;
"Speech delivered before the Whig State Convention, Boston, August 16. 1854;" "Address illustrative of the Nature and Power of the Slave States, and the Duties of the
Free States; delivered at the request of the Inhabitants of the Town of Quincy, Mass.,
on Thursday, June 5, 1856, — Altered and Enlarged since Delivery;" "Remarks on the
Letter of the Hon. Rufus Choate to the Whig State Committee of Maine, written in
answer to a Letter of the Hon. John Z. Goodrich," 1856; "Whig Policy Analyzed and
Illustrated," 1856. The Memoir of Grahame was prepared at the request of the Massa-
chusetts Historical Society, and published in their Collections, Third Series, vol. ix.
His "Memoir of John Quincy Adams" was also written at the instance of this Society.

did not hesitate to express his want of confidence in the stability of our government; but he would say, on turning the
conversation to other topics, "It will probably stand as long
as I do." As, however, the political prospects of the country continued to grow darker and darker, even this hope, if
hope it might be called, began to fade away: he became
convinced that the catastrophe might come at any moment.
Amidst these gloomy forebodings, the first glimmer of light
which he saw, or thought he saw, was in the Presidential
canvass for Fremont in 1856; for, though unsuccessful, it
showed that both the East and the West were beginning to
awake to the Great Issue.* Accordingly, he threw himself
into the contest with all the unabated ardor of his soul, as
he afterwards did into that for Lincoln in 1860. When at
length the Rebellion broke out, it gave a new life to all his
old antipathies to the slave-power, heightened by a keener
sense of the social and moral evil of slavery itself. But what
most impressed him, and this too with a kind of religious
awe, was the madness of the South, forcing upon the country
that very state of things which alone would make the final
and utter extinction of slavery both possible and necessary.

For this reason, even in the darkest hour of the struggle,
neither his faith nor his courage ever faltered, as did that of
many. This abundantly appears in his "Address to the
Members of the Union Club," February 27, 1863, and in his
"Letter to President Lincoln," on the 7th of the following
September, — remarkable in themselves, and still more so

---

* The following extract from his Diary shows that he was not among those who
counselled or favored extreme measures at this time: " January 23, 1857. — Received
a letter inviting me to attend an Antislavery meeting, the avowed object of which is
the dissolution of the National Union, — an object which I consider neither wise nor
at present practicable. To all human appearance, the event is not far distant; but I
have no sense of duty calling upon me to expedite it. I am not among those who
believe that the separation of the Free from the Slave States would inevitably lead to
the emancipation of the negroes, were it possible to unite all the Free States in such
a separation. On the contrary, I believe the only hope, and that very shadowy, of
emancipation, is from a continuance of the Union."

when considered as the last solemn and public utterances of their author in his ninety-second year. He writes to the President: —

"Negro slavery and the possibility of emancipation have been subjects of my thoughts for more than seventy years, being first introduced to it by the debates in the Convention of Massachusetts for adopting the Constitution, in 1788, which I attended. I had subsequently opportunities of knowing the views on that subject, not only of such men as Hamilton, King, Jay, and Pickering, but also of distinguished slaveholders, — of both the Pinckneys, of William Smith of South Carolina, and of many others. With the first of these I had personal intercourse and acquaintance. I can truly say that I never knew the individual, slaveholder or non-slaveholder, who did not express a detestation of it, and the desire and disposition to get rid of it. The only difficulty in case of emancipation was, What shall we do for the master, and what shall we do with the slave? A satisfactory answer to both these questions has been, until now, beyond the reach and the grasp of human wisdom and power.

"Through the direct influence of a good and gracious God, the people of the United States have been invested with the power of answering satisfactorily both these questions, and also of providing for the difficulties incident to both. . . . The madness of secession, and its inevitable consequence, civil war, will in their result give the right and the power of universal emancipation sooner or later. If the United States do not understand and fully appreciate the boon thus bestowed upon them, and fail to improve it to the extent of the power granted, they will prove recreant to themselves and posterity. I write under the impression that the victory of the United States in this war is inevitable."

He did not live to see the Union restored; but his assurance of the event was entire. He even found in the delay itself a new reason for gratitude, as it could hardly fail to save the country from half-way measures, from a conclusion in which nothing was concluded, — the only thing he really feared.

Old age, as we generally find it, is a dubious blessing; in Mr. Quincy it was singularly honored and happy. A

fall, when he was on the verge of ninety, injured his hip, so
that afterwards he could not walk without assistance. Excepting this, he seems hardly to have known, from early childhood, what is meant by sickness or physical disability. To
the very last, his bodily and mental faculties, his sight and
hearing, his animal spirits, his interest in public affairs, in
his family and friends, and even in the courtesies and ameni-
ties of social life, were wonderfully preserved. His heart
was as young and as brave at ninety as at thirty. And
these facts are the more worthy of record, as they were
manifestly the result of a strict observance of the laws of
health. They show, moreover, that where these laws are
properly attended to in other respects, nothing needs be apprehended from intense and long-continued activity of body
and of mind.

The respect felt and manifested for Mr. Quincy in his last
years by the whole community was alike honorable to both.
Party triumphs and party defeats, with the passions awak-
ened thereby, were forgotten: all that the people knew, or
cared to know, was, that they had among them a venerable
man, who had passed through a long public life without having the uprightness of his intentions questioned in a single
instance, and without a stain on his private character. Who
that was present will ever forget the spontaneous enthusiasm
with which the whole audience arose to welcome him on
occasion of his last two public appearances at Cambridge?
But the evening, however tranquil and beautiful, must have
its lengthening shadows, its setting sun, its gathering gloom.
During the summer the ancestral home in Quincy, and during
the winter his house in Boston (first in Bowdoin Place, and
afterwards in Park Street), continued to be resorted to by
distinguished strangers and devoted friends, more and more
eager to testify their regard; but the companions of his
youth and of his early manhood were not there.

From the time of his leaving Cambridge until he was

ninety, he amused himself by keeping a full journal of
events, and of his own reading, both of which led to abundant and characteristic reflections on the present and the
past.* As might be expected, the entries are often like
the following : —

"January 18, 1847. — Attended the funeral of the Hon. John Davis,
aged eighty-six years. Mild, amiable, affectionate, possessed of every
virtue. His life useful; his death easy and timely. Farewell, my
friend of many years : our separation will be short. I shall soon be
with you, and I doubt not we shall meet amidst *locos lætos sedesque
beatas.*"

"February 25, 1848. — I have to record the loss of the friend of my
youth, of my manhood, and of my old age, John Quincy Adams, who
died at the Capitol, in Washington, on the 23d instant, — on the spot
where his eloquence had often triumphed, and where his worth and
powers were known, and are now acknowledged. Death, which shuts
the gate of envy and opens that of fame, has at length introduced him
to the rewards of a life of purity, labor, and usefulness, spent in the
service of his country. The language of sorrow and lamentation
is universal. No tongue but speaks his praise, — well deserved, but
hardly earned by a life of unceasing labor and untiring industry.
Friend of my life, farewell. I owe you for many marks of favor and
kindness; many instances of your affection and interest for me are
recorded in my memory, which death alone can obliterate.

' Multis ille bonis flebilis occidit,
Nulli flebilior quam *mihi.*' "

This death was soon followed by another which touched
him more nearly. His wife, who for more than half a century had shared all his thoughts and cares, and from whom,
since his constrained absence in Washington, he had scarcely
been separated a single day, closed on the 1st of September,
1850, a long, useful, and happy life of seventy-seven years.

---

* Almost every page bears witness to the pleasure Mr. Quincy continued to take
in his classical studies. The Diary begins, indeed, with a free translation of " Cicero de
Senectute;" and Cicero, Horace, and Tacitus appear to have been his constant companions to the end. His mind was evidently of the Roman cast.

10

All his children, two sons and five daughters, survived, —
three continuing to live with him, and relieving him from all
domestic cares; the others being settled in the neighborhood,
and in a condition to render him the most delicate and grate-
ful attentions. But he could not forget those who had gone
before, and often spoke of the long-expected, long-deferred
summons to join them, with a cheerfulness and naturalness
which showed that his thoughts were equally at home in both
worlds. At length the summons came. He died, peacefully
and without suffering, at his house in Quincy, on Friday after-
noon, July 1, 1864, aged ninety-two years and five months.
The funeral took place on the following Wednesday, at Ar-
lington-street Church in Boston, his place of worship in the
city.

In looking back on this brief and imperfect memoir, what
strikes us most of all is the degree of efficiency and success
attained by the subject of it in the widely different and ap-
parently incongruous spheres of activity to which his life was
devoted at successive periods, — first as a statesman and parliamentary orator, then as a civil magistrate, and finally as
the head of a college. The elder President Adams, who was
his neighbor and kinsman, and had known him intimately from
childhood, used to say, that he "was the most fortunate man
he had ever known in his long life, — fortunate in his ancestors, in his position in society, in his wife and children, in
every thing; indeed, the most remarkable instance of good
fortune he had ever met with in his wide experience."
These words, uttered nearly fifty years ago, continued equally
true of him to the last, — most fortunate of all in a cheerful
and active old age, in a peaceful death, and an unspotted
name.

After what has been said, a formal analysis of Mr. Quincy's
character is unnecessary. He threw a vast amount of per-
sonality into his outward life : so that to know his history is
to know the man, — his excellences and his defects. To this

statement there is, however, one exception, on which it will
be proper to say a word.

His religious character was entirely misconceived by those
who were willing to regard him as a partisan for a particular
creed or sect. In the division which took place among the
Congregationalists of Massachusetts, in the early part of the
present century, he sided with the Unitarians; but he was
not a man to lay much stress on theological speculations, or
on ecclesiastical differences of any kind, or even on religious
emotions or sympathy. With him religion consisted in bringing the desires, intentions, and thoughts into harmony with
the Divine will. A man was a Christian, no matter what
might be his denomination, just so far as, at home and abroad,
in public and private life, he acted out Christian principles;
and no farther.

"Religion," so he writes in his Diary, "is an act of the mind, and
has no reference to place. It consists in studying our daily relations
to God, and in endeavoring to discern and be obedient to his will;
and in cultivating in our minds a constant sense of his goodness and
protection, and of the gratitude due to him for the infinite mercies of
which he is the source." . . .

"No years of my life have been more unqualifiedly joyful, than
those since my seventieth year. I have lost many friends and com-
rades. They have indeed gone a little before me; but what of that?
I shall soon be up with them. And I doubt not I shall join them,
and that we shall travel on together in a future life; and this temporary separation will be but an incident, and not a cause of serious
regret. This assured expectation is a never-failing source of comfort
and happiness to the well-balanced mind of an old man." . . .

"Whatever is conformable to nature ought to be regarded as
good; and what is more conformable than that old men should die?
When death happens to the young, they seem to yield to an external
force; but the old pass voluntarily away, as if by their own will.
To me the approach of death is rather pleasant than otherwise. I
seem to see land after a long navigation."

Who would not have the evening of his days made tranquil

and bright by like memories and prospects, by a like calm, natural, and sincere trust? The wonder is, that, while his faith had almost become vision, he continued as indifferent as ever to the doctrinal and ritualistic controversies which have done so much to vex and divide the Church, and indeed to all outward tests of piety except obedience and character. One who knew him well has said, " While his moral constitution kept him from all false display, the structure of his mind, as it seems to me, compelled him to bestow his attention on the logical and practical, rather than on the sentimental, aspects of religion. He went as far as he saw reason to go, and there paused, in submission to an ignorance inseparable from the present conditions of our being."* What he thought of the use and necessity of the Christian revelation, to society and government, is best expressed in his own memorable words: "Human happiness has no perfect security but freedom; freedom, none but virtue; virtue, none but knowledge; and neither freedom nor virtue nor knowledge has any vigor or immortal hope, except in the principles of the Christian faith, and in the sanctions of the Christian religion."

---

* Dr. Gannett's " Discourse, occasioned by the Death of the Hon. Josiah Quincy," p. 15.

www.ingramcontent.com/pod-product-compliance
Lightning Source LLC
Chambersburg PA
CBHW030010030726
47499CB00008B/2986